I'm waiting for y

Melodie's provocative v
Cole's head, and he nearly groaned as every
muscle in his body responded to her brazen
invitation. Her flattened palms traveled along
his shoulders and around his neck, causing her
soft, lush breasts to rasp across his chest and her
thighs to press against his. One step closer and
she'd have ample proof that he was ready, willing
and able to indulge in carnal pleasures with her.

Unable to take another moment of her bewitching
seduction, he grabbed both of her hands to regain
control of the situation and backed Melodie up
against the wall behind her.

"Dammit, Mel," he growled, his low, rough tone
threaded with frustration and desire. "You're
playing with fire."

Cole had expected her to back off, but this sexy
new Melodie was proving to be more than he
bargained for.

Instead of retreating, she let out a deep breath and
rubbed her breast against his chest. Looking up at
him with a challenge in her gaze, she said, "But
Cole, maybe I *want* to get burned...."

Dear Reader,

I think most of us are good girls at heart, with urges to be impulsive and naughty at times. And Melodie Turner, the heroine of *A Shameless Seduction,* is no exception. She's lusted after her boss, Cole Sommers, for years, and she's finally decided that she's going to shed her sensible image and have him, no-holds-barred. What ensues is a shameless seduction filled with erotic encounters, provocative fantasies and enough heat to singe your fingertips! Cole doesn't stand a chance against this female's methods of persuasion. So turn the page and discover just how far Melodie will go to get her man.

I hope you enjoy Cole and Melodie's sizzling story. And don't miss the fireworks when lady-killer Noah Sommers meets his match in *The Ultimate Seduction,* a November 2002 Blaze title. You can check out my Web site at www.janelledenison.com for updated information on both books.

Enjoy the heat!

Janelle Denison

P.S. I love to hear from my readers. You can write to me at P.O. Box 1102, Rialto, CA 92377-1102 (send a SASE for goodies!), or at janelle@janelledenison.com.

Books by Janelle Denison

A SHAMELESS SEDUCTION
Janelle Denison

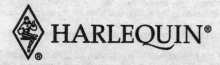

HARLEQUIN®

TORONTO • NEW YORK • LONDON
AMSTERDAM • PARIS • SYDNEY • HAMBURG
STOCKHOLM • ATHENS • TOKYO • MILAN • MADRID
PRAGUE • WARSAW • BUDAPEST • AUCKLAND

This is dedicated to all the good girls out there
who've taken chances, seduced the man of their
dreams...and lived happily ever after.

And to Don, for letting this good girl take a chance
on him. You're my happily-ever-after.

ISBN 0-373-25988-3

A SHAMELESS SEDUCTION

Copyright © 2002 by Janelle Denison.

Visit us at www.eHarlequin.com

Printed in U.S.A.

1

"I NEED A WOMAN."

"You most certainly do. Maybe if you got laid every once in a while you wouldn't be so uptight at the office."

Cole Sommers shot his younger brother a tolerant look from across the expanse of his polished oak desk. "Ha-ha, very funny, Noah. You're a laugh-riot."

Noah chuckled despite Cole's unhumorous tone. "Hey, it's the truth. Sex does wonders for a guy's attitude. Take me for example. I'm always in a great mood." His trademark bad-boy grin made an appearance, making his blue eyes gleam with satisfaction and purpose. "And judging by your surly attitude lately, I'd say it's been a while since you've blown off some...steam, among other things."

Cole grunted in reply. Reclining in his chair, he rolled his shoulders, inwardly admitting that he had been tense and restless lately. He just wasn't sure if it was a result of *not* getting laid, or rather the culmination of some unstimulating sex. The last brief affair he'd had nearly six months ago hadn't been all that mind-blowing and had left him feeling like something crucial had been missing...like an emotional connection. As a result, he'd become more discriminating when it came to dating and sexual relationships, which had narrowed the field of women considerably and left him celibate and even more irritable than normal.

But with no woman constraining him he could concentrate full-time on his true love. His P.I. firm was his mistress, and Sommers Investigative Specialists was demanding enough to occupy his days and nights.

"You're awfully quiet," Noah said, breaking into his thoughts. "Does that mean I'm right?"

"Hardly," Cole drawled. "Love 'em and leave 'em is *your* motto, not mine."

"Hell, you don't even love 'em." Noah stretched his long, jean-clad legs in front of him and clasped his hands behind his head. "That's the whole problem, Cole. For you, work comes before pleasure. It's always been that way."

"I've had my share of relationships," he refuted. But Noah was right about his dedication to his work. The wealth of responsibilities he'd taken on at a very early age was all he'd ever known. He wasn't complaining. He loved his job and career. So, at the age of thirty-three, he'd pretty much resigned himself to being a confirmed bachelor, and he was fine with that status. Work and past obligations had consumed him, a single-minded trait that stemmed from the bitter divorce of his parents, his mother's tragic death and then the loss of the one man he'd always looked up to and thought of as his own personal hero.

Unerringly, his gaze shifted to the eight-by-ten picture of his father hanging on the wall in his office. In the candid photo, his dad was dressed in his police uniform and Cole was standing next to him, a beaming young teenager without a care in the world. That had been years before his father had been shot in the line of duty and Cole's entire life and future had shifted in a way that he'd never, ever expected.

Cole's strict work ethics had been borne out of sheer preservation—for him and his younger siblings. Yet despite the burden and duties he'd accepted as his own, he'd never resented the choices he'd made. He'd like to believe that the past had made him a stronger, better man—albeit one without as great a sex life as his carefree brother.

"If you'll remember correctly, I was left with a family to support at the age of twenty-one," he reminded Noah. "That didn't exactly leave a whole lot of time for play."

The mention of their father's death sobered Noah and softened his features. "You did a damn fine job with me and Joelle. And you've spent the past ten years building this investigative firm into a reputable agency. Hell, we're all gainfully employed because of you. So maybe it's time you put a little fun and excitement into your life and enjoy whatever comes your way."

Cole grinned wryly. "Is that your answer to everything?"

"Most things, yeah," Noah admitted unabashedly. "The fun balances out the stress. Wanna place a bet here and now that I live longer than you?"

"Because of all that great sex you're having?"

Noah's grin broadened. "I'm telling you, Cole, you really ought to give it a shot—on a regular basis, that is."

A frustrated breath eased out of Cole. "Do you think we can get past dissecting my sex life?"

Noah smirked. "You mean your nonexistent sex life."

"Thank you for reminding me of that. Repeatedly."

"Hey, us guys have to stick together. You've spent a whole lot of years looking out for me, so I'm trying to repay the favor."

Cole shot his brother a pointed, direct look. "Can we get back to the *original* discussion?"

"Sure." Noah sat up straighter in his chair, affecting a serious demeanor. "Let's see, you need a woman and you think I can supply one for you. Is that it?"

Cole cringed when his secretary, Melodie Turner,

walked through his open office door just in time to
hear Noah's outrageous comment. Her deep brown
eyes grew wide with surprise, which quickly ebbed
to curiosity as her gaze slid from Noah to Cole. She
studied him with a look of feminine interest that
made his skin prickle and the heat of awareness settle deep in his belly.

He shook off the subtle reaction and damned
Noah for putting thoughts of sex into his head.
Dressed in a conservative navy dress that covered
her from neck to calves, and with her hair in a neat
and tidy French braid, his prim and proper secretary was the last woman to inspire lustful thoughts.
Or so he'd been trying to convince himself for the
past few months.

She was pretty enough in a fresh, wholesome
kind of way, but she wasn't even close to being the
type of woman he'd favored since graduating from
college years ago. Melodie was too sweet, innocent,
and nurturing for his tastes. A quintessential good
girl who looked prime for the prerequisite 2.5 kids,
dog and house in the burbs. After raising his brother
and sister, he wasn't in a hurry to repeat the process
with kids of his own, if at all. Cole had no desire to
be tied down. He liked his freedom—to come and
go as he pleased, to stay as late as he wanted at the
office—the only responsibilities being those he in-
flicted upon himself.

If his own personal credo wasn't enough to give

him a much needed jolt of reality, then there was the important fact that he'd hired Melodie two years ago as a favor. His efficient secretary was the only child and daughter of Richard Turner, who'd been his father's sergeant and best friend, and had become Cole's mentor after his dad's death. The elder man had been grateful that his little girl had accepted the position at the Sommerses' agency and was working for a man Turner highly respected and trusted.

Cole stamped that as a mantra in his brain, certain Richard wouldn't appreciate knowing he'd entertained a fantasy or two of peeling off those buttoned-up dresses from his daughter's body and finally getting an eyeful of the curves he suspected hid beneath the loose material. He'd often wondered if her breasts were as full and lush, and her legs as long and sleek, as he suspected. And did she wear serviceable cotton underwear, or lacy, silky lingerie that hinted at a softer, feminine side?

His brother cleared his throat, intruding on Cole's private musings. He jerked his gaze back to Noah, who wore a goofy grin on his face.

Cole shifted in his seat, realized he was semi-aroused, and experienced a moment of disgust. What the hell had gotten into him? Christ, maybe he *did* need to get laid as his brother had suggested—especially since provocative thoughts of his secretary were beginning to distract him more and more lately.

He'd left his door open because his conversation with Noah wasn't what he'd consider a private one. Melodie had been in his office plenty of times when he'd discussed a confidential case with his brother or Joelle. Her knowledge of his clients and cases was what made her such an exceptional, proficient secretary.

Keeping that in mind, he did his best to ignore her presence as she walked across the room to his oak cabinet to put away a client file and other paperwork. He figured she would become familiar with the Russell case quickly enough. As soon as he talked to Noah, he planned to hand over the contract and initial statement he'd taken from Elena Russell, so she could type up the report for him before he began the investigative process.

Inhaling a deep breath to clear his mind, he refocused on his brother. "Let me give you the details of the case from the beginning, so you quit jumping to wrong conclusions," Cole said meaningfully. Leaning forward, he opened the file on his desk and scanned the information he'd jotted down earlier that morning. "My client, Elena Russell, owns a shop in Pacific Heights which deals primarily in selling antique jewelry and rare collectibles she's acquired from collectors and estate sales."

"Pacific Heights?" Noah interrupted, then followed that up with a long, low whistle. "That's a ritzy part of town. What's a rich girl like her doing hiring a middle-income agency like ours?" he joked.

Cole had asked Elena the same thing, albeit a bit more tactfully. "She wanted someone outside of her social set to make sure her request for investigative services was kept as private as possible."

"Did you tell her that's why we're called *private* investigators?" Noah drawled with amusement.

Cole rolled his eyes. "I figure if she wants to throw her money our way, who am I to question her reasons?"

"Point taken. What's the name of the shop?" Noah asked, his own P.I. instincts kicking into gear.

"Heritage Estate Sales. Considering where the business is located, Elena has built quite an elite, wealthy client base over the years and has earned a reputation for the quality of the antiques and collectibles she sells, and for being fair, reliable and honest...until now."

"I take it someone is trying to besmirch her reputation?"

Cole nodded. "Yes. That would be her ex-lover, Jerry Thornton, a real estate magnate. According to Elena, during their one-year affair Jerry gave her an antique, five-carat European diamond ring that was appraised at over twenty thousand dollars. When the relationship ended, he asked for the ring back. She's holding on to the trinket claiming it was a gift, but Jerry is saying that she stole it from his collection of vintage jewelry, and he's just filed a lawsuit to that effect. He's been very public and vocal about his accusation, which has affected Elena's business and her reputation."

Noah rubbed a hand along his stubbled jaw as he mulled over the information he'd been given. "Maybe she *did* steal the ring."

"Maybe," Cole agreed, not discounting anything. "Except Elena says there's a personal letter that Jerry wrote to her that says he gave her the ring as a gift, and states that it's hers to keep forever as a token of the love they shared."

A deep chuckle escaped Noah. "A real romantic, eh?"

"Romance didn't even come close to what the two obviously indulged in. Apparently Jerry and Elena were fond of writing explicit love letters to each other, and it was in one of these erotic exchanges that he promised her the ring."

"No doubt, in the heat of the moment," his brother commented with sexual humor, which gained a small grin from Cole. "I take it she doesn't have the letter on hand."

"No, and she needs it to prove she's innocent and clear her name." From the corner of his eye, Cole watched as Melodie closed the cabinet drawer, then headed toward his desk with a stack of papers in her hand.

He absently flipped through the notes in the Russell file as she stopped beside his chair, sorting out the credit reports, invoices and contracts that needed to be reviewed and signed. She shifted and reached, and Cole caught a whiff of a soft, floral scent that wrapped around his senses and wreaked havoc with his concentration—and restraint. Her hip brushed his arm, inciting another damnable rush of heated desire he was hard-pressed to ignore.

He clenched his jaw and continued where he'd left off. "Elena claims the letter is at Thornton's hilltop mansion, tucked safely away in a monogrammed leather box she gave him for his birthday. The last she saw of the box, it was in his library."

"And she wants you to break into Thornton's house and find it?" Noah asked incredulously.

"No, she doesn't want me to break in," he shot back, his tone more irritable than was warranted. He inhaled deeply, which did little to soothe the racing pulse that Melodie's nearness had incited. "Two weeks from this weekend, Thornton is hosting a charity auction at his place for the rich and richer, and she managed to get ahold of two tickets to the formal affair. Since Thornton wouldn't appreciate her attending the event in his house, it gives me the perfect cover to get in and find that letter."

Noah shrugged. "Sounds easy enough."

Yes, at least that part of the case was uncomplicated, Cole thought. Unfortunately, Elena's *other* request wasn't as simple.

Finally, Melodie slowly moved away from him and headed for the door. He breathed a sigh of relief. "This part of the case brings me around to needing an experienced, sophisticated woman who can play up the sexy siren act as my date. A one-night, no-strings-attached kind of deal." Before his brother could issue another smart-ass remark about his sex life, he explained the stipulation Elena had insisted upon. "Since the letters Elena exchanged with Thornton are risqué and suggestive, and she's uncomfortable with a man reading what she wrote, she requested that a woman read the letters to find the one that mentions the ring as a gift."

"Ahh," Noah said in understanding. "Now I get it."

Closing the Russell case file, Cole clasped his hands on top of the folder. "Considering the bevy of females you know, I figured you could help me out. And if I could have my choice, I'd prefer if the woman who accompanies me to the charity function isn't a complete airhead."

"So you want sexy, stunningly beautiful, and intelligent." A grin quirked the corner of Noah's mouth. "Man, you don't ask for much, do you?"

Cole glanced past where his brother sat, noticing that Melodie had paused at the door. One slender hand rested on the frame and she'd cast a glance at him from over her shoulder. She'd obviously listened to the end of his conversation with Noah and was watching him in a way that made him feel way too warm. Their gazes locked, and she dampened her bottom lip with her tongue in a slow, sensuous glide that contradicted her wide eyes and guileless expression.

He felt the stroke of her tongue in places too long denied. With effort, he banished his train of thought before his body betrayed his work ethic to keep business separate from pleasure.

"Did you need something, Mel?" he asked just as the office phone rang out in the reception area.

She shook her head, causing her tidy braid to slap against her shoulder blades. Still, she didn't leave, and there was a feminine kind of longing in her soft brown eyes that added to the growing sexual awareness pulsing through his bloodstream.

"Uh, the phone's ringing," he said in a neutral tone, which finally pulled her from her daze and got her moving down the hall.

Noah sat up straighter in his chair. "That woman has it bad for you, Cole," he said in a low tone of voice.

Startled by Noah's comment, Cole frowned fiercely at him and attempted to brush off his claim. "Melodie is like a sister to me, for God's sake."

Noah laughed, a low, devilish sound. "Well, I can guarantee that she doesn't think of you as a sibling."

"How would you know?" Cole asked, keeping his composure calm and unruffled.

"You really don't see it, do you?" Noah shook his head in disbelief. "God, for a trained P.I. you sure are obtuse sometimes."

Cole didn't appreciate the insult, and refused to be baited into revealing anything his brother could use against him where Mel was concerned. "See what?" he asked, very interested in finding out what, exactly, his brother had observed.

Noah stared at him for a long, penetrating moment. "Let's see, where do I start?" He lifted his hand and began ticking off each point on his fingers. "Mel arrives early, stays late and brings you lunch when you don't go out and get something for yourself. She picks up your stuff at the dry cleaners while she's at it, runs personal errands for you and is at your beck and call for the ten or more hours a day she works at this office. Figure it out for yourself." Noah stood, once again adopting that devil-may-care attitude of his. "As for that woman you need, give me some time and I'll see what I can do for you."

"Thanks," Cole murmured as Noah exited his office.

Once he was gone, Cole jammed his fingers through his hair and dragged his palms down his face. Despite his own reaction to his secretary, and the fact that for months now he'd denied the growing attraction making itself known, he was completely shaken by his brother's observation about Melodie. And how had he missed the overt clues of *her* feelings toward him?

Cole shook his head in amazement. Obviously, his subconscious had put blinders on when it came to his secretary's interest in him.

"And they'd damn well better stay in place," he muttered to himself. Because there was no way in hell he'd ever get personally involved with Richard Turner's daughter.

IF COLE WAS in the market for a woman, then Melodie wanted to be the one to fill that role...in any capacity he might need. Even if she had to settle for a temporary, one-night date for the sake of business. Unfortunately, she had no idea how to convince her boss that she was the right woman for that job, or more importantly, the right woman for *him*.

"Dream on," she muttered to herself as she sank dejectedly into the chair behind her desk in the reception area of the firm.

She shook her head as she realized the irony of her remark. Gorgeous, sexy Cole Sommers had been a part of her dreams and fantasies for more years than she cared to recall. She'd met him for the first time when she was sixteen and her father had brought him home for dinner one night after his dad, John Sommers, had been killed. She could still distinctly remember the butterflies that hatched in her stomach whenever he glanced at her with those dark, velvet-blue eyes of his, the way her entire body tingled whenever he was near, and how her heart skipped a beat when he talked to her in that deep, smooth voice of his.

Twelve years later and he still had that same sensual effect on her. And she was still smitten, still dreaming, still fantasizing of him—and he was oblivious to her, other than her position as his faithful, efficient secretary.

Not only did she want Cole to notice her as a woman, but she'd spent the past two years at the firm trying to prove her capabilities in the P.I. business beyond her secretarial duties. She'd been intrigued by the various cases from her very first day on the job and enjoyed helping Cole, Noah and Joelle research cases—doing background checks, and learning the ins and outs of the business. Now, she was ready to take that next step, ready to show Cole that she could handle more than front-end paperwork.

Noah entered the reception area from Cole's office, and Melodie sat up straighter in her chair, shoved her personal secrets away for the time being and started thumbing through the payables she needed to process.

"Hey, sweet stuff," he said, calling her by the flirtatious nickname he'd christened her with the first week she'd come to work for the firm. "I'll be out to-morrow for most of the day working on a case, so if you need me for anything important, just give me a page."

She smiled, having always genuinely liked Noah. He was one of those men who had charisma aplenty and liked *all* women. He was, undoubtedly, a "chick magnet" as his sister was fond of saying, though Melodie had never thought of him as anything more than a friend and surrogate brother. "Will do."

He glanced at his wristwatch. "It's almost five-thirty. Why don't you take off early?" he teased, knowing full well she usually didn't leave the office until well after six most nights. "You deserve the break."

Take off early and do *what*, she wondered. Her nights were so routine and boring it was pathetic—pick up fast food on the way home, eat it while watching *Entertainment Tonight*, take a shower, slip into comfy pj's, check in with her dad, then watch TV or read a book until she fell asleep. Occasionally, on the weekend, she'd go out to dinner and movie with a friend, nothing overly exciting or wild. Then again, having been raised by a police sergeant, she'd never strayed from what was expected of her—discreet, proper behavior, in public *and* in private.

"Even Joelle enjoys the benefits of leaving on time," he said, gesturing to the office with its lights out for the evening.

"Joelle has a handsome husband to go home to," she countered.

Noah feigned a shocked look. "You mean to tell me that you don't have some hot guy waiting for you to get home at night so he can ravish you?"

Didn't she wish. She rolled her eyes at his exaggeration. "Hardly, and you're a big tease."

"Well, here's a little tip for you." He leaned close, as if sharing a well-kept secret, and gave the tip of her braid a mischievous tug. "You're not going to find Mr. Right spending all your time here."

Melodie blinked, unsure whether to take his remark as a subtle warning about his brother, a little friendly advice, or if he was just humoring her with his usual fun-loving nature.

He strolled toward the front door. "No matter how you spend the evening, have a good one, sweet stuff." With a playful wink over his broad shoulder, he was gone.

Sweet. The word grated on her sensible nerves, and her lips pursed as if she'd just swallowed something sour. She was tired of being thought of as *sweet.* Sure, being polite and courteous had its time and place, but she was beginning to realize that being amiable had gotten her absolutely nowhere with men. She'd always been prudent and modest, and as a result her life was boring, tedious and so very predictable.

She was tired of being good, of always doing the

right thing and making levelheaded choices. She had nothing substantial to show for her exemplary behavior and discerning ways—no social life other than a few close friends, no steady dates and certainly no sex life, either. At twenty-eight, she definitely wasn't having fun. She was turning into an old maid while wishing she had the nerve to be hip and contemporary, someone worldly and wise when it came to men and relationships.

Bracing her elbows on her desk, she propped her chin in her palm and allowed a smile to curl the corners of her mouth as she imagined how much fun being bad would be for a change. To break out of the monotonous pattern her life had become. To assert herself and go for what she wanted. No holds barred.

What she wanted was Cole Sommers and the chance to show him how much she'd learned about the business over the years, and the perfect opportunity had presented itself in the form of him needing a woman. She might not be sexy or a stunning beauty, but she was intelligent and knew the investigative business better than most. Certainly being familiar with the Russell case had to account for a few extra points in her favor, as well.

Excitement and anticipation rolled through Melodie as a plan formed in her mind, and when Cole entered the reception area a few moments later, she was mentally prepared to fight for this case—and her man.

"Here's the new file on the Russell case." Stopping in front of her desk, he set the folder in an empty wire basket, his demeanor strictly business. "Once you have the initial report and client invoice typed up, I'd like the file back. This evening, if possible. I have a few things I need to follow up on early tomorrow morning."

"Consider it done." Another late night at the office—by her own choice, she knew. It was a precedent she'd set of her own accord, so she couldn't blame Cole for assuming what had become routine on her part. She loved her job, but there was no denying she craved more excitement and adventure than typing up a report could provide.

He turned back around to leave, and she abruptly stood up before she lost the nerve to address him. "Cole?" His name escaped her on a breathless note.

Slowly, he faced her again, regarding her with a casual kind of directness she'd grown used to. Yet there was something in the depth of his blue eyes that made her heartbeat quicken in her chest and her knees feel weak.

"Yes?" he asked, his curt tone dissolving whatever awareness and warmth she'd seen in his expression a moment ago.

She'd never felt intimidated by Cole's size, but his presence in front of her suddenly seemed very overwhelming. He was a tall, powerfully built man and possessed a potent combination of virile strength, rugged allure and understated confidence. Lean and muscular, he was all male—from his thick, tousled sable hair, to the knit shirt that molded to his broad chest, and fitted khaki trousers that defined his hard thighs and long, sturdy legs. Definitely a candidate for the strong, gorgeous, silent type, and attracted her like no other.

A bout of anxiety knotted in her belly and her throat closed up tight. She swallowed hard, reminding herself that nothing risked equaled nothing gained—words she planned to embrace from this moment on if she didn't want to live the rest of her life like a nun. "I heard you and Noah talking about the Russell case and your comment about needing a woman to accompany you to Thornton's charity auction."

He blinked, his features taking on a curious edge tinged with a bit of caution. "Do you know someone in the business who could help me out?"

"Well, sort of." Her fingers twisted together at her waist, a nervous habit she'd developed as a young girl, and she consciously pried her hands apart and set them at her sides. "I do have a solution to your problem."

"You do?" he asked in surprise, his rich tone dropping an octave.

She nodded succinctly, inhaled a deep breath to

bolster her fortitude, and blurted, "Let me be the woman you need."

His dark brows rose a good half inch on his forehead and his entire body grew tense. "Excuse me?"

Her face flushed warmly at her slip. She hadn't meant to sound as though she was propositioning him. "For the charity auction," she rushed to clarify.

He shifted on his feet, the suggestion seemingly making him very uncomfortable. "I don't think so." His voice was low and thick.

"Why not?" She'd been taught by her father never to question or dispute a voice of authority, and while a part of her was shocked at her own outspoken behavior, she couldn't deny that the freedom to be assertive felt liberating.

Bracing his hands on his lean hips, he frowned at the subtle challenge in her tone. "Because I didn't hire you to work on cases."

"What if I *want* to work on this case?" she argued, shocking herself yet again. She pulled back her shoulders to maintain an air of confidence. "I know the business, and I'm familiar with the case. Besides, how hard can it be to pose as your date and read love letters? You need a woman for the job, and the last I checked, I definitely fulfill that requirement."

His gaze fell to her chest, and she realized that, with her shoulders back, the material of her dress was pulled tight across her breasts. To make matters worse, his heated stare caused her nipples to pucker in reaction.

He lifted his gaze back to her face. A muscle in his cheek ticked, and a harsh sigh unraveled out of him as he pushed his fists deep into his trouser pockets. "Melodie...I don't think your father would appreciate me putting you in a potentially dangerous situation."

She inwardly cringed at his placating tone, feeling anything but calm and mollified. She knew her father echoed Cole's sentiments, believing she belonged in a safe environment, free from any outside negative influences. He had, after all, suggested that she go to work for Cole as a secretary because Sommers Investigative Specialists was a respected firm run by a man her father knew and trusted. It was bad enough that she'd grown up with a father who'd spent too many years trying to shelter and protect her from any adverse situations; she didn't want or need that same attitude from Cole, or anyone else for that matter.

With that in mind, she asserted herself once again. "As a grown adult, I can take care of myself and make my own decisions. And if it makes you feel any better, my father would never have to know about me and the case."

He shook his head, causing a lock of sable hair to swipe across his forehead. "I can't take that chance...with you."

Because she was Richard Turner's daughter, she knew with a sinking feeling in the pit of her belly. As if she didn't have enough problems getting his attention, he was using her father as a barrier between them. And Cole was principled enough to stand by that decision for the next fifty years. The man was steadfast and true, and, while she admired that quality about him when it came to his job, at the moment, his tenacity frustrated the heck out of her.

She started around her desk toward him, refusing to give up or back down from what she wanted for a change. "Cole—"

He held up a hand, halting any further debate. "I'm sorry, but I won't change my mind. Your talents are better suited *in* this office, not out in the field. End of discussion."

She knew he hadn't meant his words to be condescending, but his backhanded compliment about her "talents" stung her feminine pride, especially since she knew that Cole depended on her for more than her secretarial skills. She thrust her chin out as he turned and walked back to his office. The two of them were far from finished, this issue between them far from over.

If Cole didn't have faith in her ability to be the woman he needed, she'd just have to figure out a way to prove him wrong.

2

MELODIE ABSENTLY PUSHED her lunch around on her plate with her fork, her mind too preoccupied with replaying yesterday's conversation with Cole for her to concentrate on eating the food the waitress had just delivered. While she was ready to break out of the plain-Jane, good-girl existence she'd lived all her life, she had no idea how to go about transforming herself into the kind of woman who'd catch Cole's eye.

"Don't tell me you aren't hungry," Joelle, Cole's younger sister, said in disbelief. "You're the only woman I know that has a healthy appetite like mine—I'd hate to lose that rare bond we share."

Melodie smiled at her friend and coworker from across the restaurant table. "Your appetite has doubled since you've become pregnant, Jo. I can't keep up with you and your regular bouts of hunger."

Jo rubbed her belly, which was still disgustingly small considering she was nearly five months pregnant. She wore leggings and long shirts, and hadn't even graduated to maternity clothes yet. "I have to say that being pregnant is a wonderful excuse to eat, but Dean has become such a worrier about me taking care of myself and making sure I'm eating all the right things for the baby. It's hard for me to splurge like I really want to."

Melodie laughed when Jo rolled her eyes in exasperation, but there was no mistaking the love and affection between the couple when they were together. The two had met under unconventional circumstances when Jo had taken Dean into custody in a case of mistaken identity. During the course of establishing his innocence, they'd fallen in love, though it had taken time and compromise to make their relationship work. Now, the two shared a tangible devotion and passion Melodie envied.

An exaggerated sigh escaped Jo. "He insists on making me breakfast every morning and dinner every night, with something included from all the five food groups and a huge glass of milk to top it all off. So the only time I get to satisfy my real cravings is when I don't go out to lunch with him."

Melodie twirled fettuccini noodles around her fork and stabbed a piece of tender chicken. "If the way he takes care of you is any indication, Dean will make a great daddy."

Blue eyes, identical in color to Cole's, softened with agreement. "Yeah, I know he will."

They both worked on eating their lunches, and after a few minutes of silence Jo looked back up at her and tipped her head inquisitively. "You seem distracted today, at the office and here at lunch. Is everything okay?"

Melodie took a bite of her fettuccini and debated whether or not to pull Jo into her dilemma with Cole. She desperately needed someone to talk to—a qualified, knowledgeable female who'd understand and empathize with her inexperience with the opposite sex. Melodie's mother had died before she'd ever really known her, and her father had never remarried, so she'd grown up without a steady feminine influence in her life. She had girlfriends from school she still kept in touch with, but no one she felt comfortable enough with to discuss her lackluster seduction skills.

As for Jo, well, she had a deeper insight to the man Melodie had her sights set on, so any advice she volunteered on her brother's psyche might help Mel better understand what kind of obstacles she was up against. Ultimately, she trusted Jo as a friend and confidante.

Melodie swiped her napkin across her mouth, pushed her half-eaten lunch aside and took Jo up on her offer to express what was bothering her. "Can we talk, girl to girl?" she asked, then rephrased her question. "Or rather, woman to woman?"

A grin quirked Jo's mouth and interest glimmered in her eyes. "Sure. What's on your mind?" She finished off her burger and washed it down with the last of her soda.

Melodie paused a heartbeat, then said, "I was hoping you could give me some advice on attracting a man's attention."

Jo's light, good-natured laughter rang between them. "What in the world makes you think I'm qualified to dole out advice on men?"

Propping her elbows on the table, Melodie laced her fingers together and rested her chin on top. "You snagged Dean, didn't you?"

"There were extenuating circumstances," Jo replied, brushing a wisp of blond hair off her cheek. "I certainly wasn't on a manhunt when I met him."

Melodie felt a blush sweep across her skin at the insinuation that she was interested in trawling for men. As in plural. "There's only one man I want," she clarified.

Leaning back in her padded chair, Jo regarded her thoughtfully as the waitress cleared their plates. The other woman mentioned dessert, momentarily distracting Jo with more important matters as she ordered herself a slice of chocolate cake. Melodie passed on the offer of sweets, opting instead for a refill on her iced tea.

Once the server was gone, Jo returned to her subtle analysis of Melodie from across the table. "If I had to hazard a guess, I'd say it's Cole you're after."

Melodie opened her mouth, then closed it again, unable to deny the truth. "Yes, it is," she said, relieved to finally admit her feelings to someone. "Am I that obvious?"

The waitress delivered Jo's cake and she dove right in to the dessert. "Let's just say that you have a way of wearing your emotions on your sleeve."

"Does Cole know?" she asked tentatively.

Jo shrugged. "I have no idea, though I have to say that Cole tends to shut out the things he doesn't know how to deal with. *You* could be one of those things," she added with a smile.

A frown settled on Melodie's brows. "That doesn't sound very encouraging to me."

"Knowing my brother all too well, he's probably avoiding the attraction, and if you want his attention you're going to have to force him to acknowledge it." Jo took another bite of the rich, creamy-looking chocolate cake, and took a long moment to savor the taste. "So what brought all this on, anyway?"

Melodie explained about the Russell case, along with Cole needing a woman to accompany him to the charity auction. "I made the suggestion that I go with him to the affair so I can read those erotic love letters for him. I know the case, and I've worked for him for two years doing extended background checks and researching case information. The next logical step would be for me to help him on this case, but he's adamant that my talents are better suited in the office and not out in the field."

Jo chuckled in amusement. "Oh, that's a good one."

She cringed as she remembered his unflattering comment, but wasn't about to let it deter her from her purpose. "Also, he claims he doesn't want to put me in a potentially dangerous situation, yet he's willing to use another woman as a decoy. If all that's not bad enough, he's using his close relationship with my father as an excuse to make sure he keeps me safe and out of harm's way, as if it's his duty to shelter and protect me. Between the two of them, I've had enough of being watched over."

"Wow, can I ever relate to that," Jo murmured in understanding. "Cole has always been the same way with me. He's only eased off since I married Dean. Being protective of the people in his life has been ingrained in my brother since the day my parents divorced, and that trait only intensified after our father died and he had to raise me and Noah. Cole takes his responsibilities very seriously."

"The very last thing I want is to be an obligation to Cole," Melodie said, swirling her straw through her iced tea.

Jo ate another sliver of her chocolate cake, her eyes lighting up with an idea. "If you really want to be the woman on his arm at this charity auction, then why don't you give him what he wants?"

Uncertain what Jo was getting at, she asked, "Which is?"

"A woman who fits his vision." Jo licked off remnants of frosting from her fork as she thought for a moment. "What, exactly, did Cole tell Noah he wanted again?"

"A sexy, sophisticated, intelligent woman." The prerequisite was burned in her memory.

A disarming grin curved Jo's mouth. "Then that's exactly what you give him."

"Take a look at the woman sitting in front of you, Jo," she said, her tone dry. "I'm not exactly sophisticated, sex kitten material."

"No, but you most definitely have the potential to be," Jo countered confidently. "If this is what you really want, you're going to have to be willing to play the part to the hilt. You'll need to learn to walk the walk and talk the talk, and shed a few inhibitions along the way. Think you can handle that?"

A spark of excitement flared within her. This was exactly what she needed—a friendly shove to break out of the straitlaced, conservative lifestyle she'd led for too long. "I'm certainly willing to try."

"Oh, this is going to be fun." Jo's eyes glowed with mischief. "Tomorrow's Saturday. What do you say you and I plan a girls' day out and do the works, from head to toe? Haircuts, manicure, pedicure and a few new outfits?"

Melodie's spirits lifted as she envisioned the new and improved her. "Just so long as Dean doesn't mind me monopolizing your day."

"Are you kidding?" Jo brushed off her concern with a wave of her hand. "He'll reap the benefits."

She exhaled a deep breath. "Then consider it a date."

Jo leaned across the table, her expression filled with glee. "Come Monday morning, you'll knock Cole's socks off."

Among other things, Melodie hoped. She grinned at Jo and said, "Let the transformation begin."

BY SUNDAY EVENING Melodie decided that being sexy and sophisticated entailed a whole lot of hard work. Talented beauticians had managed to transform her into a woman she hardly recognized as her former self—from the cut, color and style of her hair, to her subtly made-up face, all the way to the pale pink polish on the nails of her fingers and toes. Salesladies with an eye for flattering outfits had given her a whole new look. Coupled with Jo's approval and coaxing, her wardrobe now consisted of the kind of form-fitting and stylish clothes she'd always admired on other women but had never bought for herself.

Outwardly, she had to admit she looked like a whole new woman, the kind of worldly, wise and attractive date Cole needed on his arm in two weeks. Now she had to work on the "inner her," and all the personality traits that came with being bold, confident and assertive.

Luckily she'd been blessed with a good amount of intelligence, she thought wryly as she crawled into bed, or else she'd be in big, big trouble, because she doubted there was a trained professional she could hire to implant a quick dose of brilliance. And to her credit, she already knew the P.I. business, and the details of the Russell case. So, she figured she was as ready as she'd ever be.

Fluffing her pillows against the headboard of her bed, she propped herself up, made herself comfortable and grabbed the book she'd left on her nightstand the previous evening. The book was chockfull of sexy, provocative advice on being aggressive and uninhibited. *The Good Girl's Guide to Being Bad* covered everything from walking the walk and talking the talk, as Jo had put it, to how to tease, flirt and seduce a man with a glance or a touch. The book was all about breaking good-girl rules and embracing sensual, bad-girl pleasures. Later chapters included advice on enjoying every aspect of hot, erotic sex with the man of her choice, and how to make him a slave to her every desire.

She absorbed every page, every written word, and put it all to memory. By the time she'd finished the book it was nearly midnight, and there was no doubt in her mind that bad girls had the market cornered on fun. She'd also realized how to use an erotic letter of her own to show Cole she was a grown, sensual woman who could handle the Russell case, as well as him.

A smile curled her lips. Her fun would start tomorrow morning at the office, and she couldn't wait to see the expression on Cole's face when he laid eyes on her.

COLE WALKED INTO the office Monday morning and came to an abrupt halt in the reception area when he caught sight of a woman going through the case files in the drawers behind Melodie's desk. Startled, he cast a quick glance around the area for his secretary, but she was nowhere in the vicinity.

Frowning, he quietly moved forward, wondering what the woman was up to—was she searching for information on a client case? And where was Melodie? He'd seen her car parked outside, so she had to be in the building somewhere.

His mind considered the odd scenario while more masculine instincts took note of the way the woman's fitted lavender skirt clung to her trim backside. The hem ended midthigh, drawing his gaze to long, shapely legs covered in pale, shimmery stockings. He'd yet to see the woman's face, but there was no denying she was a knockout from the neck down.

Banishing those wayward thoughts, he stopped in front of Mel's desk and cleared his throat to get the other woman's attention. "Excuse me, can I help you with something?"

She whirled around and pressed a hand to her chest in surprise. "Cole!" Melodie exclaimed breathlessly. "I didn't hear you come in!"

Cole stared at the gorgeous vision before him, unable to believe his prim, proper and very reserved secretary had somehow metamorphosed into this head-turning, stunning creature. His mind reeled and his body felt as though he'd been delivered a punch to his midsection.

Gone was the long, tidy braid his secretary always wore, replaced by a tousled, shoulder-length cut that framed her face in soft waves and looked sexy as hell. Cinnamon-hued highlights had been added to her brunette hair, causing the silky strands to shimmer with the simplest movement of her head. The subtle application of makeup on her face brought out threads of bright gold in her brown eyes he'd never noticed before, and her lips were slick with a glossy shade of lipstick that reminded him of a succulent peach—one he wanted to gently sink his teeth into and taste...*badly*.

The knot in his stomach tightened, yet he couldn't stop staring. The cream silk blouse she wore clung to her full breasts in a way her other outfits never had and was buttoned just low enough to give him a glimpse of a creamy swell of flesh. She'd tucked the hem into the trim waistband of her lavender skirt, giving her a sleek, sexy, well-put-together kind of look. The woman had the kind of lush curves that warranted a second glance, and all these years she'd hidden them beneath loose dresses and conservative outfits.

Still shocked, his mouth opened to say something, anything, but no words emerged.

She laughed, the soft, throaty sound unlike anything he'd ever heard in her tone before. "What's the matter, boss?" she asked as a slow, sensual smile lifted her lips. "Cat got your tongue?"

The proverbial cat not only had his voice, but his groin seemed to be just as affected by her transformation. If he'd thought he'd been fighting his attraction to her before, he currently felt as though she'd launched a full-out assault on his libido, and his restraint!

He shook his head, hard, and tried to regain his composure. "What's with..." Unable to grasp the appropriate word when his mind was muddled with arousal, he gestured from the top of her head to the three-inch heels on her feet with an impatient wave of his hand. *"Everything."*

"It's the new me," she replied, and twirled around, giving him a 360-degree view of her very feminine assets. "I was in the mood for a change. What do you think?"

The problem was, he *couldn't* think, at least not with any part of his anatomy located above the belt.

Mind-blowing was the first word that came to mind, followed by provocative. With that crushable hair, those luscious lips and those endlessly long legs, she was his most carnal fantasy come to life.

Although it seemed crazy, he wondered if their conversation last week about her not accompanying him to the charity auction had instigated this radical transformation in her. Not that he had any intention of changing his mind about her doing the job.

He swallowed to ease his parched throat. "You look..." *Amazing, tempting and too damned beddable.* "Really nice," he forced out blandly.

Some of the confidence glimmering in her gaze dwindled, and he experienced a mixture of relief and regret for bursting her enthusiasm. But the last thing he wanted to do was encourage her brazen behavior in any way. He was already having a difficult enough time with his body's response to this new and sensual Melodie.

So, instead, he focused on business. "Any calls this morning?"

She hesitated for a moment, then straightened her shoulders once again, as if attempting to rebolster her fortitude. Reaching across her desk, she gathered a few pink message slips and handed them his way, her movements slow and unhurried instead of quick and efficient, as was her usual manner.

"Lance Keesling returned your call from Friday," she said, and even her voice sounded lower, huskier, to his ears. "Jonas Goodwin would like an update on the Williams insurance fraud case, and Bobby Malone will be stopping by later this afternoon with the information you needed on the MacGregor custody case."

He nodded succinctly. Bobby Malone was a detective with the Oakland P.D., and also a good friend of Noah's. The two of them traded professional favors on cases when needed, and Cole was waiting for crucial information on a prior felon embroiled in a custody dispute with one of his clients.

"Great," he said, glancing back at her after reviewing the messages she'd taken for him. "Could you pull the Goodwin case file for me and bring it to my office, please?"

"It's already on your desk," she replied efficiently.

"Thank you." At least some things hadn't changed, he thought gratefully. Despite Melodie's new attitude and alluring appearance, she was still the same old reliable, conscientious secretary he'd come to depend on in the office.

And that's all he cared about, he told himself firmly.

"Good morning, everyone," Noah's deep, cheerful voice sounded from behind Cole as he entered the reception area, followed by a quick inhalation as he obviously caught sight of Melodie. "Holy sh—" he cut himself off. Cole turned to see his shocked outburst replaced with a wolfish grin. "Who in the heck is this impostor? Certainly not our sweet Mel!"

A pink blush swept across her cheeks, but something much more mischievous flickered in her eyes. "Maybe I'm her naughty twin."

"Oh, I like that," Noah said with a too-charming laugh that grated on Cole's nerves. Noah circled around the desk, grabbed Melodie's hand, spun her in a circle for a full inspection, then made a low, growling sound of approval and appreciation. "You look incredible. I think I need to modify 'sweet stuff' to 'hot stuff.'"

She beamed up at him. "That would definitely go with my new image."

"Hot stuff it is," Noah confirmed, winking playfully at her.

An odd tension settled down the nape of Cole's neck and he was loath to acknowledge its source. Noah had always been a shameless flirt when it came to *all* women, yet Cole didn't care for the way his brother was eyeing Mel's newly revealed attributes he, himself, had ogled earlier.

He clenched his jaw in frustration and issued a stern internal lecture. He'd never been a jealous man when it came to the opposite sex, and he didn't intend to start now with a woman he had no business lusting over.

"I'm glad you came in early, Noah," he said,

drawing his brother's gaze back to him. "Can I see you in my office for a few minutes?"

Noah let go of Melodie's hand and nodded. "Sure." He followed Cole down the short hall to his office, then dropped into one of the chairs in front of his desk. "What's up?"

Taking his own seat, Cole rolled his shoulders to ease the taught muscles stretching across his back. "Do you have time this week to do some surveillance work?"

"Yeah, I can wing it. What do you need?"

"It's for the Russell case. I'd like you to tail Jerry Thornton and see if he's involved with another woman and uncover whatever you can regarding his credibility." Withdrawing a piece of paper from his blotter, he pushed it across his desk toward Noah. "Here's his home and work address and a photo, along with other pertinent info."

Resting an ankle over the opposite knee, Noah gave the notes a cursory glance, then slanted Cole a furtive look. "Speaking of the Russell case, your sexy, sophisticated, intelligent candidate for the charity auction is standing in the other room."

"Who? Melodie?" he asked, his tone infused with a plausible amount of incredulity—he hoped.

Noah smirked. "No, her *naughty* twin."

"Forget it," he told his brother firmly. "I refuse to cross *that* professional line with my own secretary."

"In order to cross a professional line you need to

be attracted to her," Noah drawled, insinuating as much. "Come on, Cole, she's perfect for what you need."

Cole's *needs* were making themselves known with a vengeance. Since the moment he'd laid eyes on Melodie's newly revealed bottom and long legs, his body had been clamoring for a more physical kind of contact. A languid dose of desire had settled beneath his skin, a nagging ache he feared would get much worse if Melodie continued her beguiling performance.

"And it's not as though you have to sleep with her," Noah added wryly.

Oh, but he wanted to, Cole thought, no longer shocked by his sinful thoughts where Melodie was concerned. Too easily, he could envision her sprawled on his king-sized bed, his own aroused body covering hers as his fingers sank deep into her silky hair and his mouth tasted her lips, her neck, her breasts. Oh, yeah, he *wanted*, and there was no sense in blatantly tempting himself with what he couldn't have.

"Look, I refuse to put Melodie in that kind of position." Or himself for that matter. "If, for some reason, something on the case goes wrong, I don't want to risk losing a damn good secretary."

Noah looked as though he was struggling not to burst out laughing at Cole's ridiculous excuse, but managed to keep his expression composed. "Whatever you say." Standing, he pocketed the information Cole had given him on Jerry Thornton. "I'll get right on the surveillance and let you know what I find out."

Cole nodded succinctly, grateful that he was no longer under his brother's scrutiny. "Thanks, I appreciate it."

Once Noah was gone, Cole deliberately buried himself in follow-up work on current cases to keep himself occupied and busy. Unfortunately, his secretary had more distracting matters in mind. Every time she walked into his office to deliver paperwork or discuss a case report with him, his gaze strayed unerringly to her swaying hips and shapely legs as she glided toward his desk in a slow, tantalizing stride. More times than he cared to admit, he caught himself staring at the soft roundness of her breasts beneath her blouse and had even witnessed a sensuous glow in her eyes when he dared to meet her gaze. Hell, even his ears perked up when she answered the phone, just so he could listen to her speak in that soft, husky tone of voice that matched her alluring packaging.

He was completely and totally aware of Melodie, in every way imaginable. Just as she'd intended, no doubt. And with every inviting smile she cast his way, coupled with a few accidental brushes of their bodies as they passed in the hallway, she added fuel to the fiery flame burning deep inside him.

By the end of the workday, he was tied up in knots, and so mentally and physically aroused he was ready to come out of his skin with a mere whisper of a touch.

The now familiar swishing sound that accompanied Mel's approach down the hall to his office put his unruly hormones back on full alert. With effort, he tamped down his eager response, and by the time she'd entered the spacious room, he'd schooled his features to reflect casual interest.

It had been blessedly quiet for the past hour. At a quarter after six, the front-end phone was silent, and both Noah and Jo were gone for the evening— which left him all alone with Melodie. His muscles tensed at the realization. Normally that wouldn't be a cause for concern, considering more often than not she worked late with him, but that was before she'd turned herself into an impudent minx.

"Can I run something by you, Cole?" she asked, her tone as serious as her expression.

Ahh, business he could handle. A piece of paper in her hand legitimized her request and made his shoulders relax again. "Sure. What is it?"

"A letter." Instead of taking one of the chairs in front of his desk, she came around to where he sat and settled herself on a cleared spot of polished mahogany to his left. "One I'd like to read to you, if that's okay."

She crossed one slender, stocking-clad leg over

the other—in the same prim and proper way she'd done a hundred times before while taking notes for him on a case. Except she'd never sat on his desk in such a brazen manner, and she'd never worn a skirt so short it ought to be deemed illegal for all the wicked, decadent thoughts it inspired.

He leaned back in his leather chair to put much-needed distance between them. "Is this for a case?"

She appeared momentarily nervous, which quickly ebbed into an adorable look of persever-ance. "Yes, it is."

Curiosity edged out the caution nagging at his conscience. "All right. Let's hear it."

Her chest rose and fell as she inhaled a deep breath, then her thick lashes lowered and her gaze dropped to read what she'd written on the piece of stationery in her hand. "You've been in my thoughts all day long, and now we're finally to-gether," she began, her soft voice at first quivering and unsteady. "I've caught you watching me when you think I'm not looking and it excites me to know that I've captured your attention, and that you might possibly want me as much as I've wanted you. Your gaze drifts over me, as soft as a caress and as warm as a sultry summer night, making me heady with breathless anticipation."

Certain he wasn't prepared to hear the rest of her letter that was taking on a very provocative slant, he offered up a protest to stop her. "Mel..."

"Shhh, let me finish," she scolded gently, though there was no mistaking that reading her erotic letter out loud was taking a huge dose of courage on her part. She shifted on his desk and slowly recrossed her legs, the movement echoing the restlessness stringing his nerves and body tight.

"You've become my sensual awakening, and now my body hungers for the intimacy of your touch." Lifting her hand, she feathered her fingers along the pulse fluttering in her throat and gradually skimmed her hand downward to the vee in her blouse as she continued to mesmerize him with her words *and* actions. "I ache to feel your strong hands stroking my cheek, my breasts and heating the soft skin along my stomach and thighs. My heartbeat quickens at the thought of experiencing such exquisite pleasure, and even now I'm trembling deep inside, waiting, hoping that you'll be the one to ease the intense longing that grows with every passing second."

She brushed loose tendrils of silky hair behind her ear, and her tongue darted out to dampen her bottom lip, making her mouth glisten like a ripe, juicy peach. "Wrap me in passion and desire, and I'll expose my every need. Tease me, please me and make my fantasies come true." She lifted her smoky gaze to his, her dark irises rimmed in brilliant gold. "I'm waiting for you. Make me yours."

Cole was so caught up in her sensual monologue

that, in his very vivid imagination, she was already his. And his invigorated body echoed the sentiment. There was no doubt in his mind that she was attempting to shake up his composure and shamelessly seduce his mind, his thoughts. And her ploy was working, considering he could only think of one thing: fulfilling hot, illicit fantasies. Hers, and his own. Together.

The temptation to touch her was overwhelming, and it took monumental effort to resist the urge to reach out and place his hand on her silky leg and smooth his palm up her thigh, then beneath the hem of her skirt. To find out if she was just as aroused as she'd made him.

He clenched his hand into a tight fist on the armrest of his chair and asked as calmly as he could manage, "Where did you get that letter?" His voice sounded gravelly to his own ears.

She tipped her head, causing her softly layered hair to sway over her shoulder and along her cheek, beckoning him to test the luxurious texture of those strands with his fingers. "I wrote it today, during my lunch break. What do you think?"

"You definitely earn an A for creativity," he replied without thinking.

A satisfied smile made an appearance on her glossy lips. "It was easier than I thought to write the letter, even kind of fun, but I was more concerned about reading it." Her gaze held his, pulling him into the guileless pools of deep brown staring intently at him. "Did I do okay?"

Any better and he would have embarrassed himself with how turned on she'd made him. "You did fine, Mel." Feeling too damned stimulated, he stood up and paced to the window on the other side of his office, then turned to face her again. "Is there a point to why you feel compelled to read me such a personal letter?"

"Of course there's a point." She slipped gracefully from the surface of his desk and glided toward him, a mixture of nerves and determination mingling in her gaze. Stopping in front of him, she placed her hand on his chest, right over his rapidly beating heart, then slid her palm upward until her trembling fingers toyed with the collar of his shirt. "I'm trying to prove I can be exactly what you need."

Oh, he needed all right. With a vengeance. In a way that was quickly zapping his common sense and rigid control. "Care to explain that comment?" he asked, shoving his hands deep into his pants' pockets.

"I'm applying for the position of your date for the charity auction." Her fingers grazed the opening of his knit shirt, scorching his flesh with her daring caress. "I know you could probably find someone sexier and more alluring," she said, a bout of insecurity showing through her bravado. "But you already gave me an A for reading my erotic love letter. Considering that's what you need a woman for on the Russell case, that skill has to count for something, doesn't it?"

"So, that's the reason for your metamorphosis and that letter you just read?" he asked incredulously. "The Russell case?"

"Partly, yes." Her chin lifted, adding a willful air to her demeanor and a new, intriguing dimension to her personality—a strength and tenacity he couldn't help but admire. "I've been sensible and accommodating all my life, Cole. A quintessential good girl, a perfect daughter and a quiet, dependable secretary. I'm twenty-eight years old. I want to have some fun and be a little wild and adventurous. And I want to find out what it's like working on a case outside of the office. I'm more than qualified, and I can help you on the Russell case, if you'd just give me the chance."

"No." His response was automatic; it was also his last link to his own personal salvation when it came to her.

"I'll do whatever it takes to prove I'm capable of handling this assignment. *Anything* at all." Undaunted by his refusal, she stepped closer, and whispered daringly, "Tease me, please me and make my fantasies come true," she recited from the erotic letter.

I'm waiting for you. Make me yours. The provocative

words echoed through his head, and he nearly groaned as every muscle in his body responded to her audacious display. Her flattened palms traveled along his shoulders and around his neck, and she swayed toward him, causing her soft, lush breasts to rasp across his chest and her thighs to press against his.

Unable to take another moment of her bewitching actions, he grabbed both of her hands to regain control of the situation and backed her up against the wall behind her. He pinned her wrists beside her head with his splayed hands and glared down at her, doing his best to discourage her advances with his dark look.

"Dammit, Mel," he growled, his low, rough tone threaded with frustration and desire. "You're playing with fire."

He'd expected his intimidation tactics to coerce her into backing off, but this new side to Melodie was proving to be more than he'd bargained for. Instead of retreating, she inhaled a deep breath and gazed up at him challengingly. "Maybe I *want* to get burned."

Oh, hell. When and how had the focus of the conversation shifted to *them?* The flush of excitement on her cheeks backed her claim, yet he instinctively knew she hadn't considered the repercussions of what she was asking for, or the fact that he wasn't a forever kind of guy. One step closer and she'd have ample proof that he was ready, willing and able to indulge in hot sex and carnal pleasures with her. But work and personal ethics kept him from following through on the primal urges raging within him.

He bent his knees, lowering his face so he was looking directly into her eyes—putting him a breath away from kissing her. "You're not ready for this kind of game," he warned in a deep, gruff voice. "And if you're not careful, you're gonna end up getting hurt."

"I'm a consenting adult, Cole," she said, blatantly ignoring his advice and jumping right into the fire. "Why not let *me* be the judge of that?"

3

HEAT LICKED through Cole's veins and spread throughout his entire body. Between listening to the erotic letter Melodie had just read to him and being on the receiving end of her daring remark to play with his brand of fire, Cole felt pushed beyond the edge of his restraint. Unable to resist the temptation he'd been fighting all day, and determined to show her just how ruthless he could be when issued such a direct and wanton challenge, he lowered his head and took her mouth with his own—finally releasing all the pent-up desire clawing its way to the surface.

His lips slanted over hers, hot and hungry, demanding even. When she gasped in startled surprise at the intensity of his kiss, he took advantage of her soft, parted lips and slid his tongue deep inside, tasting her incredible warmth and a honeyed sweetness that was uniquely hers.

With her wrists pinned beneath his hands and her head braced against the back of the wall from the pressure of his mouth on hers, he was in complete control and able to maneuver her to his will. Not that she was resisting any part of his sensual assault, though her response was far more reserved than he'd expected considering how forward she'd been with him moments ago. He was used to aggressive women who took charge in appeasing their own needs when it came to sexual encounters, yet he was feverishly turned on by Melodie's gradual awakening, and he was the one who felt mindlessly seduced.

Tentatively, she touched her tongue to his and moaned deep in her throat at the silky contact. The sexy, guileless sound vibrated through him like a physical caress, while the heat and aroused scent of her beckoned to his baser, more primitive side. Instinctively, he closed the distance between them, gradually pressing his hard body against hers and fitting his erection snugly between her thighs. He gyrated his hips slowly, rhythmically against hers and felt the entire length of her shiver with the same need swelling within him.

Forgetting that he'd meant to shock her into retreating, he released her wrists to frame her face between his palms and angled her head for better access. His lips gentled, and he slid his tongue inside her mouth again, this time slow and deep—the same way his body ached to take hers. Threading his fingers through her thick, luxurious hair, he feasted on her lips and teased her with damp, open-mouthed kisses that coaxed her to do the same, and if the soft, mewling noises she was making in the back of her throat were any indication, he was pleasing her just fine, too.

Cole's mind spun with keen sensation and an overwhelming pleasure unlike anything he'd ever experienced before. Everything about her was addictive—the feminine smell of her skin, the feel of her lush curves scorching him and her uninhibited response as he smoothed a hand down her neck, over the wild pulse beating at the base of her throat, and lower still until he cupped her generous breast in his hand and squeezed the tender swell of flesh. She arched shamelessly into his touch and moaned when he dragged his thumb over the tight nipple straining through the flimsy material of her bra and blouse.

Her cool fingers delved through his hair, tugging him intimately closer as her mouth opened wider beneath his in a giving, trusting gesture. It was that startling thought that finally jolted him out of the fog of lust clouding his brain and ruling his hormones. This was *Melodie,* and her father trusted him to look after her, yet here he was, nearly betraying the man who'd done so much for him.

He jerked back, breaking their embrace. Breathing hard, he stared down at her flushed face, unable to believe he'd been so caught up in the erotic fantasy she'd woven with that damnable letter that he'd forget his duties and responsibilities.

Unable to believe, too, just how badly he wanted to be the man she'd created on paper.

Her lashes fluttered open. Meeting his gaze, she touched the tips of her fingers to her kiss-swollen lips. *"Cole."* His name escaped on a breathless whisper of sound that belonged in a moonlit bedroom. *His* bedroom.

She looked so incredibly sexy, so beautifully aroused, and it took every ounce of effort he possessed to contain the driving impulse to shove her skirt up around her waist, crush her body with his own and take her right here, right now, up against the wall.

He took two huge steps back before he did just that, putting her far out of his reach. In a voice still holding gravelly nuances of desire, he said, "I strongly suggest that you leave for the night before we do something we'll both regret later."

She shook her head, opposing his statement, causing her mussed hair to tumble around her shoulders. "I don't think regret is possible, for me anyway," she replied softly.

A long moment of silence passed between them, making it abundantly clear that he had nothing left to add to the conversation. With a soulful sigh, she headed toward the door, but halted before stepping through the threshold. He didn't turn around to look at her, but that didn't stop her from addressing him one last time.

"Just in case there's any doubt in your mind, Cole, *I* wanted that kiss," she said in that new and brazen way of hers. Then she was gone.

Cole exhaled hard, but the release did nothing to ease the conflicting emotions of need and guilt raging inside of him. He never should have touched Mel, not even to prove a point or discourage her advances. But once his lips had glided across the silky texture of hers, there was no denying he'd wanted that tongue-tangling kiss just as much. Hell, truth be told, he yearned for a helluva lot more than just her eager mouth beneath his, and she'd felt every inch of his *yearning* pressing between her thighs.

Dropping into the chair behind his desk, he let out a snort of disgust. The biggest joke of all was on him, because she hadn't been one bit intimidated by his dominance or sexual aggression. Hadn't been at all dissuaded from her single-minded purpose to beguile him. If anything, she'd reveled in her new-found sensuality and had used it to shatter every one of his good intentions.

Her ploy had worked too well. And now that she'd begun an all-out campaign to become the woman who would accompany him to the charity auction for the Russell case, he knew he was in trouble.

Big trouble.

"HEY, HOT STUFF," Noah said to Melodie as he came out of his office and into the reception area late the following day. "I'm outta here for the evening."

Melodie shifted her gaze from the accounting fig-
ures on her computer screen to Noah, just in time to
catch him checking his wristwatch. "Hot date tonight?" she teased.

A sly smile curved one corner of his mouth. "I
never kiss and tell," he said, and winked at her, giving her the impression that he was, indeed, off to see
some woman. "Do you happen to have the
MacGregor case file?"

"Actually, I do. I was getting ready to update billing and the MacGregor case is on my list." She shuf-
fled through the pile of work on her desk, searching
for the client file. "Do you need it?"

"Actually, Cole does."

She glanced up at Noah in curiosity. "If you
haven't noticed, Cole hasn't been in all day," she
said wryly. And she had a sneaking suspicion that
last night's heated encounter between them was the
reason he'd made himself so scarce.

"Yeah, I've noticed." Noah scowled, seemingly
annoyed with his brother's absence at the office.
"I'm the one who's been dealing with him on the
phone all day long, and let me tell you, something
has him in a surly mood."

Cole was using his cell phone, Melodie assumed,
because he hadn't called through the office line.
Which also explained why Noah had collected
Cole's message slips throughout the day—he no

doubt was relaying client calls to his brother so Cole didn't have to talk to her.

Noah heaved a put-out sigh. "Cole asked me to drop off the file at his house so he could review the case report tonight. He has an appointment with the client in the morning."

Melodie stood as an idea struck. "You know what, you seem anxious to be on your way, wherever that may be," she added with a grin. "And I'd be more than happy to drop off this file to Cole on my way home."

"Really?" Noah's tone was hopeful and grateful at the same time.

"Yes, really. It wouldn't be the first time I've played courier for the business." She even had a key to his place that she'd used on occasion to deliver paperwork or some other item when he wasn't home. "And unlike you, I don't have any plans for the evening."

"Thanks, Mel. I owe you one." Noah came around her desk and gave her a smacking kiss on the cheek. "You're an absolute angel."

Little did Noah know, the plan she'd suddenly formulated to use this situation to her benefit was far more devilish than angelic. And if anything, she owed *him* for the golden opportunity he'd just given her.

Noah strolled toward the door and turned at the

last minute to flash her a charming grin. "By the way, hot stuff, nice outfit. Go get 'em, tiger."

He let out a low growl that made her laugh. She glanced down at the leopard-print cotton tank top she'd paired off with a brown suede skirt. She couldn't help but wonder if Cole would appreciate the outfit just as much as his brother had, especially since she'd worn it with Cole in mind.

Regardless of what Cole's reaction might have been to her new outfit, Noah's compliment lifted her spirits and restored her confidence. There was no denying that Cole's brush-off last night had stung her feminine pride, but his reaction to her reading the erotic letter to him, along with their kiss, had soothed her ego. And it made her realize how those written fantasies could work in her favor to seduce Cole.

Besides, what kind of bad girl would she be if she allowed him to continue to avoid her and the attraction between them? The old Melodie would have heeded Cole's subtle warning to back off, but she refused to cater to his demands when the kiss they'd shared contradicted his attempt to remain aloof.

And, oh, what a kiss it had been. She shivered at the memory of finally being possessed by Cole—his hot, seeking mouth, his skillful hands, and the press of his hard, aroused body against hers. He'd drugged her with the erotic sensation of his lips and tongue meshing with hers, and she'd melted with the heat and passion and hunger he'd unleashed.

Even now she could recall the heavenly feel of his palm cradling her breast and the exquisite way he'd flicked his thumb across her sensitized nipple. She'd been overwhelmed by the intense throb that had settled in the pit of her stomach, surprised by the yearning that rose within her—which was abruptly eclipsed by a stark emptiness when he'd abruptly pulled away from her, then insinuated that he regretted the embrace.

From some place deep inside that she hadn't known existed, she'd gathered the fortitude to set him straight, to make sure that he knew she was a willing participant every step of the way. Not that her assurance had made any difference at all to Cole, who'd obviously berated himself for taking things so far.

She'd gone home last night frustrated, and even more intent on breaking through those personal ethics of Cole's that kept her neatly categorized as a "responsibility." And while pondering the situation, she came to the conclusion that her erotic letters were the means to seducing Cole and showing him that she was not only unshockable, but a woman with a very sensual side. She'd witnessed his reaction as she'd read the letter, and knew those fantasies were the key to their relationship and a way to force him into acknowledging the attraction between them.

She wasn't about to give up after one rejection.

Neither could Cole avoid her forever.

A secretive grin curved her mouth as she cleaned off her desk and shut down her computer. Unable to fall asleep last night, she'd stayed up well past midnight penning more erotic letters of her own, all starring Cole Sommers in the role of her fantasy man. She had them in her purse and had planned to slip them to Cole at opportune times during the day. She hadn't had the chance to put her idea into action, but the possibilities were endless for tonight's impromptu visit. No respectable bad girl would pass up the chance to seduce her guy's mind and make him hot and bothered in the process. And she was determined to prove her capability of handling the Russell case until he had no choice but to admit she was the perfect candidate for the job. And the perfect woman for him.

Satisfied with her plan, she grabbed the MacGregor case file and locked up the office for the evening. She slipped into her compact car and, after stopping at Vince's deli for a quick take-out meal, headed to Cole's. A half hour later, she knocked on his door and waited anxiously for him to answer.

The door swung open abruptly, and she was completely unprepared for the gorgeous, breathtaking sight that greeted her—a shirtless Cole wearing a pair of faded jeans slung low on his narrow hips with the top button unfastened, as if she'd caught him right in the middle of undressing.

Oh, wow. She'd always known he had a wide, solid chest, but seeing it naked was a treat. So she allowed herself a few moments to enjoy it. His upper body was toned with muscle, as was his lean belly. Fascinated by the soft, silky hair bisecting his abdomen and swirling around his navel, she followed the intriguing path lower, until it disappeared into the waistband of his jeans. Her mouth went dry as her gaze settled on the impressive bulge straining the fly of his pants, and her stomach fluttered with sheer excitement and awe. The man was so incredibly male—every part of him.

"Mel? What are *you* doing here?"

She jumped at his brusque tone and immediately lifted her gaze back to his face. He was scowling at her, and judging by the annoyance flashing in his eyes, he'd been expecting Noah, and he wasn't at all happy that she'd filled in for his brother.

And then the awful, deflating possibility crossed her mind that he might have female company waiting inside for him. She forced herself to ask, "Umm, did I catch you at a bad time?"

He crossed his arms over his chest and shook his head. "No, I was just on my way out to sit in the hot tub for a little bit."

"Alone?" she ventured to ask.

He raised a brow at her personal question and very hesitantly answered, "Yes, alone."

Relieved, she flashed him a bright smile. "Well, good, because I only brought dinner for two. Me and you." Without waiting for an invitation to enter his house, which she was certain was not forthcoming, she slipped past him and headed toward the kitchen, take-out bag in hand.

"Dinner?" he echoed from behind her, confusion deepening his voice.

"I thought you might be hungry, so I stopped by Vince's on the way over and picked up a quart of potato salad and your favorite sandwich—a hot pastrami." She cast a glance over her shoulder and caught him looking at either her swaying hips or her bottom outlined in soft suede. "And for me, ham and cheese on sourdough."

He dragged his searing, blue-eyed gaze back up, his expression both tormented and troubled, which pleased her immensely. "Mel..."

Hearing the distinct warning in his tone that had the potential to lead to a speech about all the reasons why she shouldn't be there, or worse, another rejection, she turned around and graced him with a sweet smile and her familiar efficient manner. "Oh, and by the way, here's the MacGregor file that you wanted." She presented him with the client information, disappointed to see that he'd refastened his jeans on the short walk to the kitchen. At least his naked chest was still all hers to admire.

Tentatively, he reached out and took the file, careful not to let their fingers touch. "Why didn't Noah deliver it as I asked him to?"

She set the bag of food on the dinette table and hooked her purse over the back of a chair. "Because he seemed to have better things to do and was anxious to be on his way."

"So he sent you?" he asked in a way that insinuated that Noah had dumped the request off on her in order to get a head start on his own evening plans.

"No, Noah didn't *send* me," she clarified, not wanting Noah to catch any flak for something that had been her idea. "I offered and he accepted. I told him it wasn't a problem, since I've dropped things off for you before. And it isn't a problem," she assured him, then tilted her head speculatively and added, "or is it?"

Her question was direct and meaningful, one she instinctively knew he wouldn't back down from answering. Knowing Cole, there was no way he'd outwardly admit that he couldn't handle the attraction between them. And it was that bit of pride and masculine ego that she was counting on to work in her favor.

He didn't disappoint her. "No, of course it isn't a problem," he said gruffly. Tossing the file onto the kitchen counter, he speared his fingers through his thick hair and exhaled a long, slow breath as his gaze once again met hers. "Thank you...for delivering the file, and for dinner."

Satisfaction curled through her and she bit back a smile. "You're very welcome. For both. Do you mind if I join you?"

He kept his distance and eyed her warily, studying her, giving her the impression he was thinking of last night and wondering what trick she might have up her sleeve to seduce him this time around. There was absolutely nothing tucked up her *sleeve*, but the erotic letters in her *purse* were another matter altogether.

When he continued to look at her as if he didn't completely trust her motives, she tried to lighten the moment. "Despite the leopard tank top I'm wearing, I promise I won't bite."

"The thought never crossed my mind," he said too quickly.

She almost laughed, knowing he lied. But she wasn't about to contradict him and jeopardize the precious leeway she'd made with him so far. "Then you don't mind if I stay for dinner?"

"Suit yourself," he said with a casual shrug, then headed into the service part of the kitchen and opened the refrigerator. "What would you like to drink?"

Tearing her gaze from the smooth muscles flexing

across Cole's back as he moved, she opened the paper bag from the deli and withdrew their sandwiches and a tub of potato salad. "I'll take any kind of soft drink you've got."

He returned with a cola for her, a beer for himself and two paper plates.

"Ahh, paper plates. A sign of a true bachelor," she said with an indulgent grin as she set his pastrami sandwich on his plate and gave him a big scoop of the potato salad.

"Makes for easy cleanup." He slid into the chair at the opposite end of the table from her and unwrapped his sandwich.

She settled into her seat and popped open the tab on her cola. "No wonder you don't have dirty dishes stacked in your sink."

"I've always hated doing dishes, or any other housework for that matter, so I'm always looking for ways to make my life easier in that way." He lifted his beer to his lips for a drink.

She was gratified to see him finally relax with her, and knew their light, unthreatening conversation was what was putting him at ease. "Did enough housework as a kid, huh?"

"Oh, yeah," he said as a reminiscent gleam appeared briefly in his eyes. "More than I care to remember."

Just like her, he'd grown up without a mother, and she imagined life had been difficult at times for him and his siblings. And with Cole being the oldest, most of the household chores would have fallen to him. "Well, I'm definitely impressed, because your house is always spotless."

"I have a housekeeper who comes once a week," he admitted after swallowing a mouthful of pastrami. "I'm on my own the rest of the time, which is why I'm extra careful about the messes I make."

She laughed, and his gaze met hers, filled with a warmth and awareness that tickled her tummy and stirred reminders of last night's kiss. Not ready to shatter the easy moment between them with a reminder of the attraction he was fighting, she picked up her fork for a bite of potato salad and latched onto another casual topic. "So, how is everything going with the MacGregor custody case?"

He took advantage of the switch to business-related conversation. "As good as can be expected, considering what I'm dealing with. The guy wanting custody of his kid is a prior felon, and from what his ex-girlfriend has told me, he's got an explosive temper and has no business being alone with their little boy. I'm hoping the evidence we've collected against him helps to keep her son with her and only gives her ex chaperoned visitation rights."

"That's such a sad situation," she said, feeling a twinge of sympathy for the mother who was trying so hard to protect her son—at any expense. "Then again, being fought over by two parents has to be awful for the child, too."

"It's painful for everyone involved," he said, his tone low and gruff.

She regarded him thoughtfully from across the table. "You say that as if you've had experience in the matter."

"I have." His fork stilled over his potato salad as he looked up at her, his composed expression masking deeper emotions. "My parents were divorced before my mother died."

Regret rippled through her. "I'd forgotten. I'm sorry."

"Don't be." He shrugged his broad shoulders as if the matter was insignificant, yet the slight clench to his jaw told a different tale. "It was a long time ago."

Despite his dismissive tone, she had a very strong feeling that his parents' separation had affected him more than he was willing to admit. To himself or to her. "I can attest to the fact that growing up without a mother is extremely difficult, but having divorced parents has got to be just as traumatic—unless, I suppose, it's an amicable split."

"It wasn't," he said succinctly, and took a long drink of his beer before continuing. "My mother was having an affair and divorced my father for the other guy, whom she married. If that wasn't enough of a shock for my father to deal with, my mother fought for and won custody of Joelle, who was five at the time, and took her to Arizona to live with her and her new husband."

Melodie stared at Cole in stunned disbelief. Mothers gaining primary custody of their children during a divorce wasn't unheard of, but to only fight for one child seemed odd to her. "Just Joelle?"

"She's the only one my mother wanted," he said, unmistakable traces of bitterness threading his deep voice.

Her heart constricted with compassion, which she kept to herself, knowing Cole wouldn't appreciate her expressing such a sympathetic emotion on his behalf. "What about you and Noah?"

"We lived with my father, which is exactly where we wanted to be since my mother wasn't exactly the nurturing type." He pushed his fork through his potato salad but didn't take a bite. "At the time of the divorce, Joelle was only five and very confused about what was happening to her and the family. It was extremely tough to stand by and let my mother take her away from us when we knew she only wanted Jo to hurt my father even more than she already had. And her ploy definitely worked, on all of us, not that she cared that her two sons were affected by her actions."

Melodie set aside her half-eaten sandwich and exhaled a slow, deep breath, blown away by all she was learning of Cole's tumultuous past. "I take it Jo came back to live with you, Noah and your father when your mother died?"

"Unfortunately, it wasn't as simple as that. My father had to fight for custody of Joelle again, this time against my mother's new husband." His mouth twisted with an ironic smile. "Peter held on to her for a good six months, until a judge ordered him to return Jo to my father because he had no rights and he wasn't her legal guardian."

"Wow, I had no idea." She tucked her loose hair behind her ear and tipped her head. "Between your parents' divorce and your mother's and father's deaths, you've been through a lot, haven't you?"

"I'd like to think I managed okay, despite my less-than-ideal childhood," he said a bit defensively. "And my sister and brother turned out okay, too."

"You did a great job, Cole," she told him softly, sincerely. "With Jo and Noah, and even for yourself."

"That's because I had a lot of people who helped me out along the way, your father especially." Finished with his dinner, he swiped a napkin across his mouth and tossed it onto his plate. "I owe him more than I can ever repay for taking me under his wing after my father's death. He's the main reason I've done so well with my investigative business, thanks to the connections he set me up with in the beginning."

"He thinks very highly of you," she said, wanting to reassure Cole of her father's unconditional support.

"The respect is mutual."

Which was the crux of her problem between her and the man sitting in front of her—that admiration was ingrained so deeply for Cole it interfered with the attraction between them. "Yeah, I know," she said on a sigh.

Long, silent seconds passed between them, until Cole cleared his throat and pushed his fingers through his thick hair. "Geez, how in the world did we get on to such a depressing topic?"

She hadn't found their conversation dreary at all, but rather very enlightening. In so many ways. She now understood the events that had shaped Cole into such a dynamic, determined man, one who was fiercely protective of those he cared about. She'd discovered a different dimension to his serious personality, and she liked knowing that there was a bit of vulnerability beneath his strength and diligence.

The shrill ring of his cell phone on the kitchen counter was a welcome interruption, one Cole took advantage of by sliding out of his seat to answer it.

He picked up the phone but didn't connect the line. Instead, his gaze sought hers. "That's probably Bobby Malone. I was expecting his call. I might be a while."

"Go ahead." She smiled, understanding that business was a priority. "I'll be fine."

Another high-pitched ring echoed in the dining area, and he added, "Thanks again for dinner."

She didn't miss the dismissal in his tone, as if he expected her to leave while he was handling the call. He picked up the MacGregor file and she watched him head down the hall to the fully equipped office he had at home. Just as he turned the corner into the room, he punched a button on the phone and answered with a curt, businesslike, "Sommers, here."

The rest of the conversation faded away as he moved deeper into the office, no doubt her presence already pushed to the back of his mind. Standing, she cleared the table and tossed out their trash, all the while debating whether to leave as Cole had indirectly suggested, or stay just to make the evening more interesting.

A sinful grin curved her mouth. Given her two options—one the kind of good-girl response she'd lived by for too many years, and the other calling to her newly evolving bad-girl tendencies—her choice was an easy one to make.

The man had to come out of his office sooner or later, she reasoned, and then the night was bound to get *very* interesting.

4

COLE HUNG UP his cell phone after talking to Bobby Malone and getting the information he needed for tomorrow's meeting. With the incriminating evidence he'd collected on behalf of Sarah MacGregor, he was confident the little boy caught in the custody dispute would remain safe and secure with his mother—permanently.

Feeling satisfied with the job he'd accomplished, he reclined in his leather chair, his thoughts drifting back to his earlier conversation with Melodie. With more ease than he would have imagined, he'd revealed the painful memories he'd shoved away long ago in lieu of the responsibilities and obligations he'd taken on at the age of twenty-one when he'd become guardian of his siblings.

He couldn't deny that it had felt good, had been an unexpected relief even, to share all that bottled-up angst. Lord knew he'd never allowed himself to express any bitterness over his mother's actions to Jo and Noah because they'd both been through enough trauma with the divorce. Certainly no other woman had taken the time or interest to coax him to talk about his childhood and teenage years. But Melodie had cared, in a way that had made it too easy for him to trust her with revelations about his past.

A part of him wished Melodie was still there waiting for him. And immediately on the heels of that intimate thought came annoyance, that he'd want her there when he was a man who enjoyed and valued his privacy and solitary lifestyle. He'd never needed a woman around to entertain him or fill the silence that descended when he was home alone, and he wasn't about to start now with Mel.

Besides, the evening had gone exceptionally well between them, better than he'd expected after last night's tryst at the office. It appeared that things were back to status quo, right where they should be.

Now, if only that reassurance would chase away the craving for something *more* that had settled deep within him after he'd kissed Melodie.

Shaking off the desire trickling through his veins, he exhaled hard and ran a flattened hand over his bare chest. With his belly full from the dinner Melodie had brought him and his mind freed of the MacGregor case, he decided to resume where he'd left off right before his secretary had come knocking on his door. He'd left the hot tub turned on, and now the appealing thought of immersing his body in the heated water and letting the jets massage his taut muscles beckoned to him.

He headed back out to the kitchen area, and, sure enough, Mel was gone...except she'd forgotten her purse, he realized with a frown as he spotted the black leather bag hanging from the chair. And then he saw a note on the table—or rather, *a letter*—penned in Mel's feminine handwriting.

Remembering the erotic details of the letter she'd read to him, his heart pumped hard in his chest in a mixture of adrenaline and excitement he had no defense against. Unable to resist the lure of what she'd left for him, he stepped closer and picked up the sheet of stationery to read the words she'd penned.

I love the feel of water against my skin, so soft and silky as it glides across my breasts, so warm and slick as it caresses my stomach and cascades along my thighs. The trickle of water makes my nipples hard, and I like the way that feels, too. When I brush my fingers over the aching tips of my breasts I can't help but moan at how sensitive they are, and how much I wish my hands were yours.

If I can't have you with me, I'll have to do the next best thing. I imagine you touching my wet, slick body in quivering, needy places. Your hands explore the sleek feel of my flesh while your mouth and tongue add to the heated moisture on my skin. Slowly, you lick the droplets from my body, the softness of your tongue adding to the exquisite sensation coiling deep inside my belly.

I'm drenched all over. Can you taste how much I want you?

By the time he finished reading Mel's fantasy, he was hard. If that provocative letter wasn't enough to drive him insane with lust, then the postscript she'd jotted at the bottom of the page certainly did the trick.

Cole, I'm all wet and waiting for you. Come join me for a moonlight dip under the stars.

He lifted his gaze from the come-hither words seducing his mind and spied her shoes, skirt and tank top heaped on the floor by the open slider leading to his backyard. He shook inside, knowing exactly where she'd disappeared to and what her tempting note implied—she'd gone skinny-dipping and was waiting for him to join her.

Oh, man. He squeezed his eyes shut and sent a silent prayer upward for the strength to resist her seductive scheme, then headed out the patio door and into the darkness of night, intending to turn her offer down flat and send her home.

Except he never anticipated that he'd be so mesmerized by the shadowy figure sitting in his hot tub, her upper body illuminated by the landscaping lights placed in strategic areas of his backyard. He stopped at the edge of the hot tub, relieved to see the straps of her black bra curving over her shoulders, indicating she wasn't completely naked under the frothing water. She'd secured her hair in a haphazard pile on top of her head with a clip, and dewy moisture clung to the exposed skin of her throat and her chest, right down to where the water gurgled and bubbled at the cleavage revealed by her skimpy bra. The rising steam from the hot tub swirled around his jean-clad legs and heightened his awareness of how slick and warm her skin must be.

Slowly, you lick the droplets from my body... Oh, yeah, he wanted to do that, and much, much more.

She cast a sultry glance up the length of his body. "I take it you decided to join me?"

He crossed his arms over his chest, doing his damnedest to maintain a nonchalant attitude. "I don't think that would be the smartest thing for me to do right at this moment."

She dipped lower into the water and swam across the short expanse of the hot tub to where he stood, causing a small wave of water to slosh over the side and splash onto his bare feet. Glancing up at him, she rested her arms on the rim of the tub and propped her chin on the back of her hands. "Maybe you ought to consider being a little impulsive. I'm discovering being spontaneous can be very liberating—and a whole lot of fun."

He didn't bite at the bait she was dangling in front of him, though he was sorely tempted. "Being impulsive can also get you into a lot of trouble."

She dipped her fingers into the heated, churning pool of water then flicked the tips up at him, spraying his chest with tiny droplets. "I'm willing to take that chance."

He was so hot and bothered, he was surprised that the moisture beading on his skin didn't sizzle. "I'm not."

She didn't seem at all deterred by his unwillingness to get in with her. "Did you like the latest letter I wrote for you?" she asked, her tone much too innocent.

"What letter?" he replied just as guilelessly.

"The one on the kitchen table." When he didn't reply immediately, she dampened her bottom lip with her tongue and went on. "Let's see if I can refreshen your memory. It went something like how I love the feel of water caressing my body and imagining your hands on my wet, slick skin—"

"I remember," he cut her off roughly, knowing he'd never be able to stand still while she recited her erotic letter to him.

An amused smile curled the corners of her mouth. "Ahh, you did read it," she teased, then grew serious. "Every word is true, you know. Especially the last part."

Gradually, she stood, slowly straightening to her

full height, and his mouth went dry as he watched the rush of water shimmer down her body. The feminine curve of her waist ended where the water began, revealing more than enough slick skin to bring her written fantasy to vibrant life in his mind. She might have been wearing a bra, but the shiny, wet material edged in black lace clung to the full swells of her breasts like a second skin, doing nothing to hide her tight, hard nipples from his gaze.

"I'm all wet and waiting for you, Cole," she said huskily.

An urgent need throbbed through him, settling bone deep and dredging up the arousal he'd been fighting to keep at bay. She was so damned bold. So brazen. So daring. It was an intoxicating combination that sent his senses reeling and pushed him to the limit of his control. If she wanted impulsive, he'd give her just that.

He wondered how far she was willing to take this act of hers, and was prepared to go along with her charade until she decided she'd had enough. He'd warned her last night that she was playing with fire, and she was about to see how it felt to get burned.

To her credit, she didn't look away when his fingers went to the waistband of his jeans and he unfastened the top button. She continued to watch as he eased the zipper down over his burgeoning erection, her lips parted, her eyes widening in fascinated awe. His blood heated at her breathless reaction to him stripping, and he forced himself to maintain a cavalier attitude when he was suddenly feeling excruciatingly turned on.

Hastily, he shoved his jeans over his hips, down his legs, and kicked the denim aside. He left his cotton briefs on—at the moment his underwear provided a much-needed barrier from her eager and very avid gaze. Hopping into the tub, he sat down on one of the contoured resin chaises, submersing his body up to his chest.

He rested his arms along the rim of the Jacuzzi as Melodie slid into another chair and stretched her legs so they nearly reached his lap. She sank deeper into the water, and sighed in pure pleasure as spurts of air and bubbles rose all around her.

"The massage jets feel great, don't they?" he asked, knowing she was experiencing a full-body effect from the small, pulsating jets situated in the seat.

She squirmed and laughed lightly, the sensual sound filling the moonlit night. "Umm, they even tickle in certain places."

The provocative image that flooded his brain nearly undid him, and by some miracle he was able to hold on tight to the reins of tonight's seduction. "It feels even better against bare skin," he told her, a deliberate dare in his tone. "You know, if you're going to go skinny-dipping, you should do it the right way to experience the full sensation of those jets massaging your entire body." Showing her just how spontaneous *he* could be, he shimmied out of his briefs and dropped them onto the cement with a wet *plop*, certain she'd be too timid to follow through on her end.

Though her bright eyes flashed with an initial bout of hesitancy, true to her newly adopted impudent personality, she proved him wrong. Biting the edge of her bottom lip in her only show of modesty, she held his gaze as she slowly slipped the straps of her bra down her arms, then removed the piece of lingerie beneath the froth of water. She tossed the soaking wet garment onto the ground to join his briefs, but left her panties in place.

"Oh, wow," she said with a gasp of startled surprise that held unmistakable nuances of delight. "You're right. It does feel incredible, like a hundred tiny fingers gliding over my breasts." She paused for a moment, her voice dropping to a husky pitch as she added, "But it's not nearly enough to satisfy the ache between my thighs."

His breath left his lungs in a harsh exhale and the heat of arousal gripped him like a vise.

Without warning, she swam across the short distance separating them, keeping her naked upper body cloaked in the swirl of eddying water as she neared. While male instincts urged him to reach out and grab her, he remained motionless, too curious to see what she'd do first, and how far she'd go in her pursuit of seducing him.

His jaw clenched as she shamelessly straddled his lap. Her knees grazed his hips and her slender thighs settled on top of his, searing his nerve endings with the mindless feel of her sleek, wet flesh caressing his. That wholly feminine part of her was inches away from the thick erection straining upward along his belly, and he thanked a higher power that she'd opted to leave her panties on, which helped to keep him honorable.

With effort, he kept his gaze on her face, flushed from the steam rising from the water and a feverish anticipation he could see glowing in her eyes. "Comfortable?" he drawled, his wry tone contradicting the tension and hunger building steadily within him. The muscles across his shoulders and arms bunched as he struggled to keep his hands planted on the rim of the hot tub.

"Very." Smiling too sweetly, she grabbed his wrists, brought his hands to her breasts and pressed his palms against her soft, pliable flesh. Her nipples instantly hardened at his touch. "I've imagined you touching my wet, slick body in quivering, needy places, Cole," she said, her trembling voice drawing him into her fantasy.

And she wanted her fantasy to become reality.

Her heart beat wildly beneath his hand, and he could only guess how much courage her words and actions had cost her. With her responsive, heavenly breasts nestled in his palms beneath the churning water, he stared at her sexy, luscious mouth, her lips so full and soft and irresistible—beckoning for him to kiss.

Damn, but he wanted her. More than he ever thought it was possible to crave a woman. He swallowed hard. If he crossed this intimate boundary with her, he'd be stepping beyond the point of no return. But he was only human, a normal, hot-blooded man who could only take so much teasing before he gave in to the kind of blatant temptation Melodie presented. So, he made the conscious decision to throw caution to the wind and deal with repercussions later.

Cursing his own weakness, he took a huge leap into the fire and captured her mouth with his. He parted her lips with his tongue, sinking deep, claiming her hungrily, ravenously. She expressed her need just as eagerly. Pushing her fingers through his hair to hold him close, she matched his desire stroke for erotic stroke.

Beneath the heated water, he kneaded her breasts in his hands and rolled her stiff nipples between his fingers, a purr of pleasure escaping from her throat. Smoothing his splayed palms lower, he blindly traced the curve of her waist, the feminine flare of her hips, and dragged his flattened palms along the outside of her thighs to the crease of her knees. Her skin felt impossibly soft, so amazingly silky, and the frantic need to kiss her elsewhere, *everywhere*, overwhelmed him.

Breaking their kiss, he buried his face into the curve of her neck and nudged her chin up with his jaw so he could suckle her soft, sensitive flesh against his teeth. She shivered, moaned and tilted her head back to allow him better access. He licked the droplets of water from her skin in long, slow laps of his tongue and reveled in her uninhibited response to his teasing caresses.

Unexpectedly, she lifted up on her knees, bringing her lush breasts out of the water so that moonlight kissed her pale, wet skin, giving him his first glimpse of her fully naked. The crests of her tightly puckered nipples were at eye level for him, and the sight sent his arousal spiking like a fever as he waited for her to make the next move.

Tangling her fingers into his hair, she tugged his head back. Their gazes locked, hers dark with honest passion and a heated yearning that begged him to have his way with her. "I'm drenched all over, Cole," she whispered raggedly. "Taste how much I want you."

Enticingly, erotically, she arched into him and brushed a velvet-soft nipple against his lips, coaxing his surrender, tempting him to sin. Unable to refuse something he wanted just as badly, he opened his mouth wide and drew her into the damp, heated depths, shuddering when she moaned, long and low. He suckled her greedily, tugged gently with his teeth, and used his tongue to lick and soothe and excite.

She gasped, her fingers flexing against his scalp, a bundle of restless, pent-up sexual energy. "Cole..." Still on her knees, she shifted and rubbed her pelvis against his belly, narrowly missing the blunt tip of his erection. "I need you to touch me."

While her words were vague about what pleasure zone needed his attention the most, her body spoke a desperate language he instinctively understood. He knew exactly where she ached, knew precisely what she yearned for. And it was her uninhibited request that made him a slave to her every whim.

Releasing her breast from the wet suction of his mouth, he watched her candid expression as he skimmed his palms up her sleek thighs and came to a stop when the tips of his fingers made contact with the edge of her panties. The fact that her lower body was still submersed in the gurgling, white-capped water made his touch more illicit.

He glided the pad of his thumb along the wet silk covering her mound, pressed deeper, and she jerked in reaction. "Are you sure this is what you want, Mel?"

Her lashes fluttered closed, and her breath came in small, anxious pants. "Oh, yes, *please*," she pleaded shamelessly.

Having gained her acquiescence, he deliberately forced her knees wider apart on either side of his thighs by spreading his legs, which also released an upward torrent of bubbles from the small jets in the seat of his chaise. Pulling the elastic band of her underwear to the side, those massage jets found a home at the crux of her thighs, tickling, teasing and heightening her need for release, but apparently not providing enough friction to push her over the edge.

"Oh, yes," she groaned and gripped his shoulders, her entire body trembling.

A few firm strokes of his thumb would have done the trick, he knew, but he wasn't about to let her have her orgasm that easily. She'd twisted him up in knots twice now with her erotic letters and brazen seduction, and it was only fair that he repay the favor.

Cupping the back of her head in his free hand, he brought the shell of her ear to his mouth and shared a fantasy of his own with her. "Imagine that every touch of those bubbles is my tongue, licking and tasting and probing right *here*," he murmured in a low, raspy tone as he swept his thumb along the swollen folds of her sex, while working a long finger inside of her, then two, stretching her to accommodate his penetration. She was tight and slick, and he groaned savagely against her neck as her inner muscles clutched at him and drew him deeper still.

She rocked her hips toward him with a needful whimper, and he thrust his fingers slowly, rhythmically into her. "Can you feel me inside of you, Mel?"

All she managed was a whimper of sound.

Doing the unthinkable, he replaced the slide of his thumb against her clitoris with the throbbing head of his penis and rubbed, eliciting a low growl of pleasure from his chest and a startled gasp from her. "You feel so damned good." And more than anything he wanted to bury himself in her heat and be a part of her orgasm when she came.

Accepting that that particular fantasy wasn't going to happen, *ever*, he instead catered to fulfilling hers. Bringing her sweet mouth back to his, he kissed her while increasing the pressure and friction of his fingers, his sole focus on her pleasure. The tremors buffeting through her body shattered, and she climaxed with a stifled sob against his lips.

With her face pressed tight against his damp throat and her arms wrapped around his neck, she lowered herself back into the churning, steaming water onto his lap, and slumped into him, utterly limp and sated.

He wished he could claim the same, but knew he was in for another long, sleepless night. With her draped over him as she regained her breath, he held her close, and then stiffened when he felt her insinuate her hand between them and curl her fingers around his pulsing, excruciatingly sensitive shaft.

He sucked in a quick inhale as her thumb grazed the burgeoning tip, and he grasped her wrist to stop her sensual assault. "No, Mel," he rasped, his protest weak, but necessary.

She glanced up at him, her brown eyes deep pools of rekindled desire, and confusion. "Don't you want—"

"Hell, yes, I *want*," he interrupted gruffly, refusing to lie when she held proof of his need in her slender hand. "But we can't make love." And he wasn't in the mood to go it solo while she watched.

"We?" she said, a frustrated note seeping into her soft voice. "I can speak for myself, Cole. I know it might be hard for you to believe, but I am a consenting adult who has every right to say yes to having sex with a man. With *you*, even."

A fact she'd made more than obvious tonight. As calmly as he could manage, he said, "Mel, I don't have any condoms with me or in the house."

He wasn't sure she believed him, though it was the absolute truth. Since his last affair months ago, no opportunity had arisen to make him rush out and buy a box of prophylactics. Now he was grateful he didn't have any on hand, because it was the only thing keeping him from making a huge mistake with Melodie.

Squeezing him in her fist, she leaned forward and

dragged her tongue from his collarbone up to his ear, and whispered, "Then why don't you let me pleasure you?"

His hips bucked in reaction, sliding his erection along her snug grip, and he swore as he nearly came. This time he pulled her hand completely away, then lifted her from his lap and set her back on one of the other seats. "You're driving me crazy," he muttered. And this growing obsession with her had to stop.

"Why is that such a bad thing?" she asked quietly.

"Because..." He plowed his fingers through his hair, dampening the strands. "Because I can't give you what you need." There, he'd said the words, blunt and to the point.

Wicked amusement danced in her eyes. "I think you just did."

He shook his head at her frank and sexual reply, still amazed that his secretary had metamorphosed into such a bold vixen. It was obvious she wasn't giving up on her pursuit, which made him more determined to be brutally honest with her.

"Physically, yes, I gave you what you *needed*, but emotionally I can't. I don't want entanglements or anything complicated, Mel. With anyone." And especially her. He wouldn't jeopardize his bachelor status or his relationship with her father for a hot night of sex with her.

She dipped lower into the whirlpool, until the water lapped over her bare shoulders. "To my recollection, I haven't asked for either, just a chance to accompany you to the charity auction for the Russell case."

He hardened his resolve and narrowed his gaze at her. "What happened tonight won't change my mind about that."

She touched her tongue to her upper lip, damp with beads of perspiration from the heat of the water, then sighed. "Then I guess I haven't been trying hard enough."

"Hard" definitely seemed to be a fitting choice of word for the evening, considering his body wasn't even close to settling down. And to think that she was intent on continuing this seduction of hers was enough to keep him permanently aroused. He felt as though he was sitting in a caldron of boiling water, ready to explode, and this conversation with Melodie wasn't helping.

Without further argument, he climbed out of the hot tub, giving her a brief glimpse of his naked backside before he dove into the adjoining pool. The startling impact of the cold water rushing along his overheated skin was just what he needed to put things back into proper perspective. Unfortunately, nothing could tame his raging hormones and the undeniable need he'd developed for Melodie Turner.

Damn her anyway, for turning his orderly world upside down.

He executed a dozen laps across the pool without stopping, releasing as much tension as possible and pushing himself to the brink of physical exhaustion. When he finally came up for more than a single breath of air, he noticed Melodie was no longer in the hot tub.

She was gone, just as he wanted.

So why did he feel so damned disappointed to find himself alone once again?

5

COLE STROLLED into Murphy's Bar and Grill after work Thursday evening and scanned the patrons sitting at the tables in the lounge area. He searched for a certain brown-haired man while nodding hellos to acquaintances and lifting a friendly hand to the owner of the restaurant, who was tending drinks for the crowd.

"What'll it be, Sommers?" Murphy called from his position behind the mahogany-and-brass bar, which gleamed proudly from nightly polishing. "The usual?"

"That would be great, Murph." Cole glanced around once more, didn't see who he was looking for, and berated himself for arriving late when he'd had every intention of showing up early. He returned his attention to the owner. "Have you seen Richard Turner by any chance? I was supposed to meet him here at seven." And much to his chagrin, it was nearly twenty-five after.

"Yep. I saw him walking toward the john." The older man hooked a finger down the hallway leading to the bathrooms as he placed a drink onto the pour pad at the end of the bar for the waitress to pick up. "He's sitting at that corner booth in the back with the empty martini glass on it. I'll send over a refill for him, too."

"Thanks." Cole headed in the direction of the table, the path through the lounge a very familiar one, as were the distinct sounds of customers playing pool and darts and generally having a good time.

Ever since Cole had turned twenty-one, he'd adopted his father's watering hole as his own hangout, mainly because he knew the regular patrons at Murphy's, most of whom had been friends or colleagues of his father's from his days as a cop. Murphy's was also an unpretentious, blue-collar establishment where he could escape to and relax after a long day at the office.

Tonight he was undoubtedly tense, and he was positive no amount of alcohol could ease the knot in his stomach and the muscles bunched tight across his shoulders. Not when Melodie's father had called him at the office to request that Cole meet him at Murphy's for a drink because he had something important to talk to him about.

Talk about what, exactly, Cole had no idea, though he'd spent the better part of the afternoon worrying and wondering. Richard had sounded troubled on the phone, enough so to make Cole a bit nervous about what was on the other man's mind that concerned *him*.

With a deep exhale that did nothing to ease the pressure in his chest, he slid onto the Naugahyde seat and settled himself in the booth to wait for Richard's return. Self-reproach had hung over him like a black cloud since the night with Mel in the hot tub, allowing him no peace of mind. While he'd managed to keep things between himself and Melodie strictly businesslike for the past two days, he suddenly felt as though every one of the sinful and erotic deeds he'd indulged in with Mel was stamped on his forehead for her father to see.

"Here's your beer," a soft, feminine voice said, a welcome interruption to his agonizing thoughts. With a friendly, tentative smile, the bar waitress set a glass of tap on the table in front of him, along with his favorite snack. "And Murphy said you always like a bowl of roasted peanuts to go with it."

"Yeah, I do." He grinned easily in return, noticing like every other guy in the place that the blond-haired, blue-eyed angel owned a body straight out of the centerfold of a magazine. She wore the requisite bar uniform of jeans and a kelly-green T-shirt with Murphy's Bar and Grill emblazoned across her well-endowed chest.

Despite her obvious attributes, she did nothing for his libido. No, it seemed he was hooked on a certain brown-eyed brunette who was all wrong for him.

He shifted his attention to her name tag, then met

her gaze, which she quickly focused elsewhere, as if she were trying to hide something. A ridiculous notion, considering he didn't even know her. "You must be new here, Natalie."

"I am," she verified as she set Richard's fresh martini on the table, then cleared off the empty glass and soiled napkin he'd left behind. "You'll have to bear with me. I'm slowly learning who the regulars are and what they like."

"Well, if any of them give you a hard time, you let me know," he said in a way that was completely lighthearted and meant to make her relax.

She laughed and tipped her head to regard him closer. "Are you a cop, too?"

"No, a P.I., but the instincts are pretty much the same." He took a quick swallow of his beer to quench his thirst, then introduced himself while pulling his leather billfold from his back pocket to pay for the drink. "I'm Cole Sommers, by the way, and you've probably met my brother by now since he's a regular here, too. His name is Noah."

Recognition flashed in her eyes, then her expression turned guarded. "Yes, as a matter of fact, I have met him. He's quite the flirt—and a great tipper." Her voice held nuances of gentle humor.

Cole wondered if his brother had tried to make a play for the beauty, and wouldn't have been surprised if Noah had attempted to work his charm on her. Except she didn't seem the type to fall for a sexy grin or a playful advance. There was a certain caution and vulnerability about her that was apparent to him as a trained investigator and he hoped Noah picked up on it and steered clear.

Opening his wallet, he withdrew a large bill and dropped it on her tray. "Keep the change, Natalie."

She lifted a brow in surprise. "Big tippers run in the family, huh?"

He gave a shrug. "I wouldn't want word to get out, especially to my brother, that I'm a *cheap* tipper."

She smiled in appreciation, though a bit of mischief touched her features. "Thank you, and I'm sure if Noah finds out that his brother has outtipped him, it'll only work to my favor."

Cole chuckled, watching the woman move on to take an order from another customer, until he caught sight of Richard heading toward their table and remembered the reason he'd come to Murphy's tonight.

He'd been summoned.

The older man slid into the opposite side of the booth and Cole immediately acknowledged his tardiness. "I'm sorry I'm late."

"No need to apologize." Richard waved a hand between them, dismissing his words. "You know I of all people understand work and last-minute crises. I figured if you couldn't make it tonight you would have called."

Cole wondered if Richard would be so understanding about the craving he'd recently developed for his daughter, then gave himself a hard mental shake. Two years ago when Melodie had applied for the position of secretary, her father had asked him to hire her on, essentially entrusting his daughter to Cole's care. She'd become a valued employee, and Richard had been content and satisfied knowing his daughter was working for a reputable, honorable man.

A bark of cynical laughter nearly erupted from Cole's throat, but he managed to keep it tamped with a swallow of beer. Oh, yeah, he was one honorable son of a bitch. He'd taken advantage of Melodie when he should have had the strength and fortitude to resist her advances.

He was quickly realizing he had no self-control where she was concerned. And that was yet another personal issue that rubbed him raw since he'd always prided himself on remaining cool and collected during any situation. And especially when it involved a woman.

Scooping up a peanut, he cracked open the shell, tossed the nut into his mouth, and chewed. "I got the impression on the phone that this isn't a normal social meeting. Is everything okay, Richard?"

"With me?" He stirred his martini with the green olive garnish. "Oh, yeah, I'm doing great."

Cole agreed that Richard looked more relaxed

than he'd seen him in a long time. "Retirement certainly looks good on you."

"It's not half bad." He grinned, his brown eyes twinkling with animation. "I spend my days cutting it up on the golf course and most of my evenings dazzling the ladies at the country club with my dance moves and witty conversation."

Cole laughed, amazed and delighted to hear that this man who'd immersed himself in his work as a sergeant for the Oakland Police Department for so many years was finally enjoying a social life of his own.

Richard smacked his lips after taking a drink of his martini, a touch of melancholy in his gaze, another contradiction to the no-nonsense attitude Cole had always known this man to possess. "You know, son, it's taken retirement for me to realize that I never really took the time to smell the roses along the way, and I overlooked a whole lot of opportunities that could have given me a richer, fuller life."

Surprised by Richard's confession, Cole merely nodded and ate a few more shelled peanuts, unsure where this odd conversation was heading. Obviously the man felt the need to talk, and the least he could do was lend a listening ear.

Richard stared into the clear depths of liquid in his glass and sighed. "After Mel's mother's death I focused my extra time on my daughter and spent all my energy on work in an effort to ease the pain of losing Lauren. I never thought I could love another woman as much as I loved her, so I didn't even bother to date. Not seriously, anyway."

He lifted his gaze back to Cole, a small frown marring his brows. "Everything I ever felt for Lauren I gave to Mel to compensate for the loss of her mother. I wanted to make sure that she never doubted she was loved, and that she was raised with the best of everything. And that included sending her to a private all-girls school so she could be around friends her own age who understood the female changes she was going through, and so she'd focus on her studies instead of being distracted by other outside influences, like boys and parties, and that sort of thing. I just wanted her to have every opportunity and advantage so she'd grow into an intelligent woman who'd make levelheaded choices in her life."

"You did an amazing job with her," Cole said, reassuring the other man. "She's turned into a very capable woman." Too capable, he thought privately, especially when it came to seducing him.

"Yeah, she has," Richard agreed proudly, though there was a thread of concern underscoring the tone of his voice. "But now I'm wondering if I didn't make a mistake in the way I raised her. She never seemed to resent my decision to send her to an all-girls high school, but I can't help but question if that didn't stifle her as a blossoming young woman, or make her feel as though she was living in a cocoon with no outside stimulation, like boys and coed parties," he added.

Cole shifted in his seat. The direction of the conversation couldn't get any stranger, though in a bizarre way it was beginning to make too much sense to him. "What brought all this on?" he asked reluctantly.

"I had dinner with Melodie last night and I nearly fell out of my chair when she walked into the restaurant to meet me," he said, running a hand through his still-thick hair. "She's cut her long hair into a fancy shoulder-length style and she was wearing a pair of pants that looked like they were made out of some kind of leather material and a top that showed..." his face flushed, and he lowered his voice as he added "...way too much *cleavage*. Hell, I almost didn't recognize her and I'm her own father!" He downed the rest of his drink in one gulp.

It was nice to know that Cole wasn't the only one who'd been thrown for such a loop by Melodie's transformation.

"Don't get me wrong," Richard continued gruffly. "Every woman has the right to make the most of her...assets, but I've never seen such a radical change in Melodie before. And it's not only the clothes and the hair. There's just something overall different about her, especially in the way she presents herself."

Oh, yeah, she was definitely more confident, more assertive, more candid. More *everything*, Cole thought.

Richard shoved his empty glass to the edge of the table for the waitress to pick up. "I'm sure you've noticed the change in her, as well."

"It's kind of hard not to," he muttered, then nearly winced when he realized he'd spoken his thoughts out loud.

Richard frowned, scrutinizing him from across the table in a way that made the back of Cole's neck heat.

"I mean, it's a drastic change so who *wouldn't* notice?" he quickly amended before Richard could see the guilt that had no doubt flashed in his gaze. "You know how unpredictable women can be. I'm sure it's just a phase she's going through."

Richard nodded sagely. "I sure as hell hope so, but I hate to take any chances that something else might be going on with her."

Cole's gut tightened unexpectedly. "What do you mean?"

"Melodie has always been a sensible girl who has made practical decisions for most of her life, and this is such a rebellious move for her." Richard's lips pursed in tempered agitation. "My biggest worry is that she's made this drastic change in her appearance for some guy. And if that's the case, who knows how far she'll go to get his attention."

Cole knew exactly what extremes Melodie was willing to go to capture *his* attention, but he wasn't about to share those details with her father. "What are you suggesting?"

Richard clasped his hands on the table and pinned Cole with a direct, businesslike look. "I need you to do me a personal favor, Cole. I want you to keep an eye on Melodie for me."

Richard's *favor* wasn't so much a request as an order, straight from a man who'd honed that particular skill as a sergeant. "You want me to tail her?" Cole asked incredulously.

"So to speak." Richard had the good sense to appear a tad sheepish, but parental instincts seemed to be driving him and he wasn't backing down. "I know Mel would kill me if she knew, but I can't help it. I'm worried about her, and you're the only one I trust to keep an eye on her and make sure some guy isn't using her or taking advantage of her."

The peanut Cole had been swallowing felt like sawdust in his throat, and he coughed to clear it away. He didn't deserve this man's trust, especially not when *he* was that potential man. "Richard, Melodie is a grown woman—"

He held up a hand to cut off Cole's lecture. "I know, I know. I've been telling myself the same thing, but as a father who adores his daughter, I don't want her to end up getting hurt, if it can be avoided. Trust me, you'll understand where I'm coming from when you become a father some day."

After spending so many years raising Noah and Jo, having kids wasn't in Cole's future agenda, so he could only take the man's word for how he'd react in a similar situation. Then he grimaced as he recalled a time or two when he'd checked up on the whereabouts of his little sister and Noah when he'd thought they were getting themselves into trouble, and he realized how ingrained that particular instinct was for him.

"I just need to be reassured that Melodie's okay and not getting herself into a situation that might be way over her head," Richard went on. "Will you help me?"

He owed this man so much, and he felt bad for even hedging over his answer. Then again, he couldn't very well refuse the job without Richard getting suspicious about his relationship with his daughter, or having to outright tell him the truth about Melodie's metamorphosis. And if Richard was concerned about his daughter being involved with a man, Cole could well imagine Richard's fury if he ever discovered that Melodie wanted to use herself as a plant on one of his cases.

Scrubbing a hand along his jaw, he dredged up the words Richard was waiting to hear, especially since *he* was the object of Melodie's pursuit. "I'll do it."

His mentor breathed a sigh of gratitude and smiled. "I knew I could count on you."

Cole finished off his beer and signaled the waitress for a refill, feeling the need for another drink. Protecting Melodie from himself would only be a matter of keeping his distance from her, but a more complicated issue arose in his mind.

Who would protect *him* from Melodie's quest to seduce him?

MELODIE'S FINGERS tightened around the pen in her hand and she nearly screamed in frustration as she watched Noah escort yet another woman out of Cole's office, through the reception area, and open the front door to see her out.

"We have a few more women to interview," he said to the leggy redhead as she stepped outside and turned to him with a hopeful gleam in her eyes. "Cole will give you a call if he decides to hire you for the job."

The redhead affected a sultry smile and ran the tip of one long crimson nail down the front of Noah's shirt. "Well, I appreciate you thinking of me, Noah. Even if I don't get the job, *you* can call me anytime."

Noah's trademark flirtatious grin slid into place. "I'll keep that in mind, Heather." He waited until the other woman was safely in her car before shutting the door and sauntering back into the reception area.

Melodie pinned him with an accusing look. Misinterpreting the source of her agitation, he held his hands up in a defensive gesture. "Hey, it's not as though I *promised* to call her."

"You're a complete rake, Noah Sommers," she said, shaking her head in mild disgust. "I fervently wish that someday some woman brings *you* to your knees."

"Many have," he said without a beat, his eyes twinkling with wicked mischief.

A warm flush suffused Melodie's cheeks, but she refused to let such a ribald comment fluster her. "Let me rephrase my comment. I hope you find a woman you absolutely have to have, and she makes *you* work for *her* affection. Some woman who'll reform you and your playboy ways."

He considered her remark for a moment, his expression changing to one of amusement. "It's a novel thought, isn't it?"

She rolled her eyes at his insinuation that no woman could tame the bad boy he'd always been. She couldn't even bring herself to laugh at his teasing statement, not when she wanted to reach out and throttle him—along with his brother.

Shoving the tips of his fingers into the front pockets of his well-worn jeans, Noah's gaze turned serious with concern. "Who or what has your feathers all ruffled today, hot stuff?"

She drew a deep breath, set her pen aside, and boldly met his gaze. "Actually, at the moment, it's *you*."

Startled shock flashed across Noah's features. "*Me?*"

"Yes, *you*," she reiterated. "You're the culprit behind all these airheaded women traipsing in and out of the office for the past two days, aren't you?"

"I'm just following the boss's orders," he said with a shrug. "Cole asked me to find him a woman that can accompany him to the charity auction and read Russell's love letters per Elena's request, and that's exactly what I'm trying to do."

Don't try so hard, she wanted to tell him, but bit her tongue, knowing that Noah truly wasn't at fault for following through on Cole's orders. At the moment, he was just an easy target for her own troubled emotions.

"Cole better choose someone, and fast," Noah went on with a distracted sigh, "because I'm running out of suitable candidates."

And Cole had made it abundantly clear that she wasn't suitable for the job, no matter how much experience she'd gained in the P.I. business over the past two years. This was her chance to do more, to be more, and he was being as stubborn as an ox. Personally and professionally, Cole refused to acknowledge just how good they could be together, and he'd shot down every one of her attempts to prove otherwise.

He knew exactly where she stood and what she wanted, yet for the past few days he'd purposely avoided being alone with her. His businesslike demeanor discounted everything that had happened between them the night at his house and made her feel she was right back where she started—being nothing more than a front-end secretary. She'd even tried planting a few of her erotic letters in his desk and in his briefcase, and though she was certain he'd read them, she'd gotten no response at all from him.

And now she'd finally had enough of being ignored when she had proof of just how much Cole wanted her. Desired her. If he could so easily dismiss her, then she damn well was going to try to do the same with him.

She glanced at the clock on her desk; it was 5:05 p.m. on a Friday afternoon and freedom beckoned, as did the rebellious urge to do something completely wild and frivolous. For once she wasn't going to spend a Friday evening alone at home, curled up in bed with a book or watching a rerun on TV while wishing she was doing something fun and exciting instead.

No, tonight she was determined to strike out on her own, put to use her newly developed bad-girl skills in the real world, and see where those naughty impulses led her.

"I'm outta here," she muttered beneath her breath. Abruptly, she stood up, turned off her computer, and started clearing off her desk.

"And just where are you off to, hot stuff?" Noah asked, obviously having heard her comment.

"I'm going to go out tonight and have a good time." Retrieving her purse from the bottom drawer, she raised her chin confidently. "Could you tell me the best place to meet men?"

Realizing what she intended, his eyes widened in a look of surprise, which was quickly replaced by a casual, humorous attitude. "Well, I don't think I can help you out with that. I'm not exactly into that kind of thing myself."

She frowned at him. She wasn't asking for a gay bar, and he knew it. "A place where *men* go to meet *women*, then."

He crossed his arms over his broad chest and tipped his head curiously. "Now why would you want to go to a place like that?"

Melodie recognized his hedging for the stall tactic it was, but refused to change her mind. "The reason should be obvious. I'm tired of always being the quintessential good girl. I want to have fun and meet men who'll show me a good time and treat me like a real woman." She dug her keys out of her purse and gave Noah a direct, no-nonsense look.

"So, you can either recommend a reputable place, or I can find a nightclub on my own."

Noah shifted uncomfortably on his feet. "You know, I really don't think you going out alone is such a good idea."

She sighed, disappointed that Noah found it necessary to protect her virtue just as much as every other man in her life. "It's a great idea, and since you don't seem inclined to help me out, I guess I'm on my own."

She started for the door, and he gently grabbed her elbow before she could leave. "All right, all right," he said, all traces of his normal, carefree nature gone. "Since I obviously can't talk you out of this crazy idea of yours, then I might as well make sure you go somewhere safe. There's a place called Paxton's—it's hip and contemporary and the security is tight there. They open at eight." Letting her arm go free, he reluctantly gave her the cross streets for the nightclub.

"Thank you," she said, appreciating his concern for her welfare, despite her own struggle to be an independent woman. If she was going to pursue the nightlife, she really did prefer to do it in a safe, respectable environment.

Pushing through the door, she gave him a jaunty wave. "Have a good weekend, Noah. I certainly plan to."

COLE ENTERED the reception area, a client report in hand for Melodie to type up, and frowned when he found the surface of her desk cleared for the evening and Noah standing by the front door staring out the window.

"Hey, where's Melodie?" he asked as he dropped the five-page report into her in-basket, thinking she'd most likely run out to get a bite to eat since it was only five-fifteen.

Noah turned and headed back toward her desk, his expression way too pensive for Cole's peace of mind. "I'm not sure you really want to know," his brother replied wryly.

Cole frowned, an ominous feeling settling in the pit of his stomach. "Why *wouldn't* I want to know?"

"Let me put it this way. Melodie's not thrilled about all the women you've been interviewing while you've been ignoring her, and she's decided that she wants to have fun and meet men who'll show her a good time and treat her like a real woman. Her words, not mine."

Cole rubbed his temples, where a slow throb was making itself known. "That doesn't tell me where she is," he persisted.

"She asked me where she could go to meet men," Noah replied matter-of-factly. "So, I told her about Paxton's."

Noah had sent her off to a trendy nightclub? Images flashed through Cole's mind, taunting him.

PLAY THE
Lucky Key Game
and you can get

Do You
Have the
LUCKY
KEY?

FREE BOOKS
and a **FREE GIFT!**

Scratch
the gold
areas with a
coin. Then check
below to see the
books and
gift you can get!

YES! I have scratched off the gold areas. Please send me
the **2 FREE BOOKS** and **GIFT** for which I qualify.
I understand I am under no obligation to purchase
any books, as explained on the back of this card.

342 HDL DNV3   142 HDL DNVR

FIRST NAME	LAST NAME

ADDRESS

APT.#   CITY

STATE/PROV.   ZIP/POSTAL CODE

🔑🔑🔑🔑 2 free books plus a free gift   🔑🔑 1 free book

🔑🔑🔑 2 free books   🔑 Try Again!

Offer limited to one per household and not valid to current
Harlequin Temptation® subscribers. All orders subject to approval.

Visit us online at
www.eHarlequin.com

DETACH AND MAIL CARD TODAY!

(H-T-07/02)

© 2002 HARLEQUIN ENTERPRISES LTD.
® and ™ are trademarks owned by Harlequin Enterprises Ltd.

Melodie dancing with other men. Melodie drinking and letting go of inhibitions. The situation was too ripe for sex and sin, and Cole was furious that Noah had encouraged her interest. "Why the hell would you go and do something stupid like that?" he barked.

Noah lifted a dark brow at his insult. "Give me more credit than that, Cole. It was the smartest move I could make considering how intent she was on going somewhere, with or without my help. She made it abundantly clear that if I didn't suggest a nightclub for her to go to, she'd find one on her own. I figured this way you'd know exactly where she was, and you could go and keep an eye on her."

Cole jammed his hands on his hips. "What makes you think I *want* to keep an eye on her?"

"Maybe you don't, then." Noah stared at him for a long, penetrating moment, then gave him a too-pleasant smile. "She's a big girl so she can take care of herself, and she's a consenting adult and can do whatever she wants, with whomever she wants."

Cole's blood pressure spiked a few notches at the thought of Melodie doing *anything* with another man. He released a harsh exhale, torn between letting her go to Paxton's unchaperoned to get the experience out of her system, and heeding Richard's heartfelt request. *You're the only one I trust to keep an eye on her*, he'd said.

Without further internal debate, Cole knew what

he had to do—what he *would* do—because he'd made a promise to Richard, and if anything happened to Melodie he'd carry that blame with him for the rest of his life.

"Goddamn it, anyway," he cursed between gritted teeth and stomped back down the hall to his office to shut everything down. After the day he'd had and the women he'd interviewed for the Russell case—none of whom even came close to what he was looking for—he didn't need this added stress with Melodie.

Noah followed and propped a shoulder against the doorjamb. "You're doing the right thing, Cole."

"As if I have a choice," he muttered as he switched off his computer and shoved files into his briefcase. Hearing Noah chuckle at his expense, he narrowed his gaze at his brother. "You're enjoying this way too much."

"Yeah, I guess I am," Noah said with an unabashed smirk. "Watch yourself with Melodie tonight. She's a little feisty and she's issuing curses," he joked.

That caught Cole's attention. "Oh?"

"Would you believe she cursed me with finding a woman who'll reform me and my playboy ways?" Noah feigned a shudder.

"Ha! Like that'll ever happen," Cole said with a cynical snicker. "That's about as likely as me settling down, getting married, and having a passel of kids.'' And he knew for a fact that that particular scenario wasn't in his future plans.

But playing protector to a stubborn, determined, sexy woman most definitely was.

6

COLE WADED his way through the throng of people jammed into Paxton's on a Friday night, the loud, pulsing sound of rock music reverberating through his tired body and increasing the pounding in his temples. Strobe lights flashed in time to the music in the dimly lit establishment, adding to the dull ache in his head and making it difficult for him to see beyond a few feet in front of him.

Without a doubt, Paxton's was the happening place to be on a weekend night, but the loud, raucous atmosphere and abundant display of female flesh was more suited to Noah's outgoing nature than Cole's low-key personality. He preferred a quiet night at home or a casual beer at Murphy's to the earsplitting music and the lascivious stares from the opposite sex.

Much to his chagrin, as he made his way through the crowd, women eyed him like a favorite piece of candy they wanted to unwrap and devour. Some were even bold enough to touch him as he tried to brush past in his single-minded quest to find Melodie. So far, he'd felt a hand slide along his arm, fingers skimming down his spine and a brazen palm pass over his buttocks. But there were so many people around him he couldn't be sure who'd done what.

He continued his search while nursing a soda, ignoring the voluptuous women in tight-fitting outfits shoving their breasts in front of his face and others who attempted to strike up a conversation, which was nearly impossible over the deafening beat of the music. And that suited Cole just fine since he wasn't in the mood for a hollering exchange of inconsequential chitchat.

Twenty minutes later, he finally spotted Melodie standing at one of the three bars in the establishment. He welcomed the rush of relief pouring through him, grateful that she hadn't decided to go to another nightclub instead of the one Noah had recommended.

She was facing the bartender as she ordered a drink, and he moved closer to get a better look at her, deliberately keeping himself concealed in the crush of patrons as he neared. The strobe lights alternately illuminated her, giving him flashing glimpses of her shiny brown hair with auburn highlights as well as a partial glimpse of the outfit she wore. The strappy dress was made of some kind of beige, stretchy, ribbed material that clung to her shape, making him wonder if she was even wearing a bra beneath the sheath. Or panties for that matter.

He certainly couldn't detect any obtrusive lines along her backside that would indicate otherwise.

Ignoring the stirring of desire smoldering to life inside him, he frowned as he caught sight of something colorful on her upper shoulder, a shape that looked suspiciously like a butterfly in flight. He blew out a deep breath as he drew the only conclusion available—she'd gotten herself a tattoo. No doubt her own personal statement of rebellion and independence.

Merging back into the crowd, he swore a colorful stream of expletives, knowing he was partially responsible for driving her to this extreme by rejecting her advances. She was turning defiant, reckless and wild, and who knew what she'd do next to prove to herself and everyone around her that she was a bold, aggressive kind of woman who could handle anything and anyone.

And it appeared she was going to make her point with the good-looking guy with sandy-blond hair who'd just sidled up to the bar next to her. Before she could open the small purse hanging from her shoulder to pay for the drink the bartender had just delivered, the other man forked out the cash to cover her bill. Her lips moved with the words "thank you," and she graced him with a sweet smile that made Cole feel as though he'd been sucker punched in the belly. He felt a slow burn of jealousy that he immediately tried to dismiss. And failed.

The other man bent toward her to say something directly into her ear, and Melodie laughed in response and nodded her head. With a hand pressing against the small of her back, the man led her to a table near the back of the club where two other guys sat and welcomed her into their group.

Seeing the potential for trouble, Cole moved to the outer fringes of the room where he could keep his presence concealed while he continued his surveillance. Alternately, he watched the guys at the table and kept an eye on her drink when one of them whisked her off to the dance floor to enjoy the entertainment.

For the next hour and a half Cole monitored the situation from afar. From what he'd observed, none of the men crossed the line with Melodie in a way that would prompt him to intervene, though he didn't care for the touches and casual caresses that passed between her and a few of the guys, or the sensual way Melodie moved as she danced that drew too many appreciative stares. While he was miserable and cranky and resenting the men who dared to touch her, she was having a great time— dancing and laughing and thoroughly enjoying herself and the company she kept.

From Cole's last count, she'd consumed five drinks and was working on her sixth, which no doubt accounted for her carefree, bubbly and enthusiastic attitude. He stared into the depths of his third plain cola on the rocks, wishing he could indulge in something stronger to take the edge off the frustration and other inexplicable emotions raging inside him.

He downed the rest of his drink, and set his empty glass at the end of the bar. When he glanced back in the direction he'd last seen Melodie, he frowned, realizing he'd lost sight of her. She was no longer out on the dance floor with the blond-haired guy who'd bought her first drink.

A huge wave of unease twisted inside him. Maneuvering his way past clusters of people, he swept the place with a shrewd glance in an effort to locate Melodie. Within minutes he'd scanned the entire area, but hadn't found her or her date. A frantic sensation gripped him and made his heart thunder in his chest, and his worst fear clawed its way to the surface—she'd gone home with the guy.

"Shit!" Dragging a hand along his clenched jaw, he looked over at the table where the other men had been sitting with Melodie, only to find all of them gone, as well. His stomach cramped even worse at all the possible, dreadful scenarios starting a mad dash through his overimaginative brain.

So much for Richard trusting him to keep an eye on his daughter! He'd taken his gaze off of her for two minutes and she'd left, intoxicated, with men she didn't even know. How was he going to explain such an unforgivable blunder to her father?

The scorching imprint of a very feminine body pressed up against his backside, and he stiffened as slender hands and arms slipped around his waist. Before he could turn around, she stood up on tiptoe, causing her full, soft breasts to rub along his spine, and whispered huskily in his ear, "Looking for someone?"

He identified the sultry voice as Melodie's, and his aroused body instinctively recognized her unique scent and lush curves and responded accordingly. Grasping her wrists, he whirled around and scowled at her, both relieved to find her safe and unharmed, and furious that she'd turned him inside out with worry for her welfare.

She swayed into him, catching her balance with her hands against his solid chest. Her soft, warm lips touched the shell of his ear, and he shuddered with awareness as her damp breath feathered against the sensitive skin just below his lobe. His heartbeat quickened, as did a certain masculine part of his body.

"You don't look like you're having a very good time," she said over the throbbing beat of the music, her throaty voice infused with a taunting amount of amusement.

"I'm having a *great* time," he forced out through gritted teeth, then pulled in a deep, rational breath. "Where's your date?"

One smooth, bare shoulder lifted in a casual

shrug. "He left with his friends to go to a different nightclub." Lashes falling half-mast, she played with the buttons down the front of his shirt, her index finger slowly making its way lower.

Shoring his defenses against her bold exploration, he caught her wandering hand and lifted it back up to his chest. "I think it's time you left, too." He'd take her home and let her sleep off the effects of the alcohol.

Her bottom lip curled into a pout that contradicted the defiant tilt of her chin. "I'm not ready to leave yet. I'm enjoying myself too much, though I think we ought to loosen you up a bit."

"I don't think so," he said gruffly.

She blinked languidly and met his gaze, her own eyes glowing a deep brown hue rimmed in brilliant shards of gold. Her hair was tousled like burnished fire around her head, and her full, glossy lips tapped into primitive and dominant male urges he was doing his damnedest to keep confined behind a facade of control.

Lifting her hand, she smoothed her fingers along his taut jaw and trailed the tips to the back of his neck, setting his senses on fire. "You look very, very tense, and I have just the cure." Her mouth curled into one of those seductive smiles that had been his downfall twice before. "Come dance with me," she beckoned.

She was a witch, and this time he wasn't about to let her cast her spell on him. "No."

The one word was spoken abruptly and loud enough that two other women cast a curious glance their way. Unfortunately, his very vocal refusal did nothing to deter Melodie from satisfying her own desires. "I want to dance, Cole. With you."

Her hand dropped to the waistband of his jeans, and she hooked two fingers into his belt loop. Turning toward the mob of people on the dance floor, she tugged at him to follow, leaving him with only two options...to accompany her, or take the risk of her ripping his pants off.

Keeping in mind how many drinks she'd consumed, he opted to follow her instead of drawing attention to them with a struggle or argument. She dragged him into the middle of writhing bodies gyrating to the provocative beat of the music. Cole had never been keen on dancing, and he decided he wasn't about to start now. He stood there in the crush of people, willing to suffer through one song so Melodie could get the urge to dance out of her system. Then he would haul her out of the place and take her home.

There wasn't much room to maneuver without bumping into someone, and Melodie took advantage of their close proximity. Encircling her arms around his neck, she drew him as close as two bodies could get with their clothes on, from her breasts all the way down to her knees, and moved against him, slowly and rhythmically, in a way that was completely, inherently sexual.

She brought his head down to hers and pressed her mouth against his ear to be heard. "Dance with me, Cole. I want to feel your body moving against mine."

Her suggestive invitation devastated his good intentions. He had no idea how she always managed to provoke him into doing things he knew he shouldn't. Just like the other night in the hot tub, he found himself giving in to her request, wanting the same thing, unable to refuse what his own body craved as well.

Splaying a hand on her lower back and cupping her hip in his other palm, he melded their lower bodies and wedged a leg between her soft, slender ones. Angling her pelvis intimately closer, he slid his knee higher, pressed deeper, pushing the hem of her dress up until she rode his hard thigh. The damp heat of her seeped through his jeans and he groaned at the incredible surge of hot, carnal lust that kicked up his adrenaline.

"*Yes.*" The single word left her lips, drowned out by loud rock 'n' roll, but he knew what that acquiescence meant, knew what she ached for, and knew he was about to take her exactly where she wanted to go. Here and now.

He rocked her tighter against his thigh, building a

slow, illicit friction that made her eyes darken with growing need. Strobe lights pulsed in time to the music, and someone brushed up against Cole from behind, but nobody paid any attention to them, nobody cared that Melodie was wrapped securely in his arms, straddling his thigh, performing her own private dance just for him.

Their scandalous behavior was reckless. Dangerous. And wildly exciting. Her lashes fluttered closed and she arched into him, gripping his shoulders for better leverage, a tighter fit. Recognizing the signs of her approaching climax, his own breathing deepened, and he started to sweat, the heat that caused it all internal. Ecstasy flitted across her expression as her head fell back, and her lips parted in the throes of supreme pleasure. Her legs clenched around his, her hips undulated, and he absorbed the shudders that rippled through her.

The moment was so erotic, so insanely arousing, yet there was no satisfaction to be had for him. At least not at the moment. While Melodie could keep her orgasm discreet in a public place, men just didn't have that kind of luxury, and his own release would have to wait until he could take matters into his own hands later.

She opened her eyes and looked up at him with a soft, content smile, and as one song segued into another, her satiated body gradually came alive again, swaying provocatively, enticingly, along the length of his. Tempting him, teasing him with what he hungered for, but couldn't have.

She turned around in his arms, aligning their bodies front to back, giving him a clear view of the bright, colorful tattoo on her shoulder. Raising her hands above her head, she shimmied her hips against his groin, inflaming him with the uninhibited tactic. He had no idea where in the hell she'd learned to move like that, but the effect ravaged his senses and destroyed the last thin thread of his control.

Muttering an expletive, he grabbed her around the waist and locked her tight against his chest, uncaring that she could feel the branding heat of his erection nestled between her buttocks. She was, after all, the cause.

"We're leaving, *now*," he growled into her ear, loud enough that she could hear him above the din. "And I'd appreciate it if you didn't make a scene."

She stiffened defiantly in his arms. "I'm not ready to leave."

And he wasn't about to let her stay so some guy could take advantage of her pliable and very sexual state of mind. "It's past your bedtime, sweetheart." Grasping her arm firmly in his hand, he wove his way through the throng of people on the dance floor, surprised that his fierce erection allowed him to walk normally. "Come on, I'm taking you home."

"I'm just starting to enjoy myself," she yelled

back as she trotted behind him in her heels while trying to finagle her arm from his grip. "*You* go home. I think I'll shut the place down."

He shot her a withering look from over his shoulder, his arousal and her resistance feeding his anger. "Like hell you will!"

Her lips pursed stubbornly, but she didn't back down from his scowl. "Nobody asked you to babysit me, Cole."

He barked out a harsh breath of laughter. "Somebody needs to make sure you don't end up passed out somewhere between here and your apartment." Or in another man's bed. The thought alone caused his blood to boil with jealousy, and he wasn't leaving *anything* to chance.

"I'm *not* drunk," she shouted indignantly.

He continued plowing forward through the crowd, his eye on the red Exit sign above the main entrance. "You're right," he tossed out to her, a sarcastic bite to his tone. "What was I thinking? After consuming six drinks in the span of two hours, of course you're not the least bit intoxicated!"

Shoving open the double doors to the nightclub, he strode out into the clear night air, his ears and head thanking him for leaving the boisterous entertainment behind.

"You can't just drag me off against my will!" Melodie shouted, her shrill tone capturing one of the bouncer's attention who'd stepped out for a smoke break.

Cole inwardly cringed as the big, beefy guy crushed out his cigarette and stepped forward to assist the woman in distress. Thinking fast, he whipped out his wallet, flashed his P.I. badge like a cop in control of a critical situation, and addressed the other man in an authoritative tone of voice. "This is my sister, and for your information she's underage and has no business being in this night-club."

The guy's eyes widened in shock. "Hey, man, I'm sorry. We card everyone who goes through that door."

Melodie glared at Cole, then tried to reason with the bouncer. "I'm not underage!"

"Not with that fake ID you're carrying, you're not," Cole drawled smoothly as he pocketed his billfold before speaking to the other guy again. "I'll let the oversight slide this time, but if it happens again, you can bet the Feds will be crawling all over this place, and I'm sure your boss wouldn't appreciate being slapped with a hefty fine."

The other guy backed off immediately, mumbling apologies, obviously not wanting to deal with the liability his "sister" presented. With a slack-jawed Melodie by his side, he crossed the graveled parking lot toward his utility vehicle.

"I can't believe you just did that," she said once

she'd shaken off her astonishment and regained her ire.

He shrugged unrepentantly. "I don't need any more trouble than what I've already got with you."

"Me?" Her exasperation raised a notch as she doubled her steps to keep up with his long-legged stride. "I was doing just fine in there until you came along."

He grunted in reply. He didn't even want to consider what could have happened if he *hadn't* shown up at Paxton's. Would she have allowed one of those guys the same liberties on the dance floor that she'd granted him? His temper flared at the thought.

Unlocking the truck by keyless remote, he opened the passenger-side door, placed his hand on the top of her head, and guided her inside the car, giving her no choice but to obey. He slammed the door shut and was halfway around the vehicle when she popped out of the vehicle again, the small purse hanging from her shoulder slapping against her hip.

"I'm not going anywhere with you, Cole," she said stubbornly, and yanked at the hem of her dress, which had ridden up on her thighs.

His jaw clenched in aggravation. Keeping his gaze off her long, bare legs, he stalked back and silently, but firmly, forced her back into the leather seat. With one hand on her squirming shoulder to keep her in place and his upper body blocking what he was about to do, he opened the glove compartment and withdrew a set of steel handcuffs he kept tucked in there for emergencies. And this situation definitely qualified. He looped the cuffs through the handgrip on the dash, then manacled one of Melodie's wrist, then the other. Then he slipped out of the car again and closed the door on the sound of her outraged gasp.

She fumed as he pulled out of the parking lot, then finally unleashed the resentment simmering inside her. "I don't appreciate you treating me like a common criminal." She gave her shackles a fierce tug, but they didn't budge.

He eased the SUV onto the freeway toward Oakland. "I'm ensuring your safety since you don't seem capable of doing it for yourself."

"This is unbelievable," she said with a slow shake of her head, then stared out the window and the darkness beyond. "What about my car?"

"We'll pick it up tomorrow. You're not driving anywhere tonight. Your father would kill me if you were picked up on a DUI charge," he muttered.

Her head whipped around fast, causing her hair to swirl around her face. The heat of her gaze bore relentlessly into him. "Excuse me?"

Damn. He shifted in his seat. If she ever learned of the conversation that had transpired between himself and her father they'd both be dead meat.

With a calm expression in place, he looked her

way. "I said, the last thing I'd want is for you to get picked up on a DUI."

Her gaze narrowed suspiciously, but she didn't call him on his comment. "I'm *not* drunk," she insisted, and rested her head against the back of her seat. "And I can take care of myself. Take me home."

That's what he'd originally planned, but wondered if he could trust her to be alone in her current rebellious mood. Would she crawl into bed and sleep off the alcohol she'd consumed after he left her apartment, or would she find a way to head back to the nightclub? The dilemma ate at his conscience.

You're the only one I trust to keep an eye on her. He groaned at the reminder of Richard's unconditional faith in him, and knew what his decision would be.

Preparing himself to deal with another argument with Melodie, he headed toward home. *His home.*

MELODIE KEPT her gaze trained out the passenger window and ignored her grumpy, temperamental chauffeur. She still couldn't believe that he'd gone to such extremes as to handcuff her, or that he thought he needed to save her from herself. Of course, Cole was under the wrong assumption that she needed protecting. And for some reason, he'd assigned himself the job of being her savior.

She released a soft sigh. Tonight wasn't turning

out at all as she'd imagined. Then again, where Cole was involved, nothing went the way she expected.

The evening had started out well enough. While she'd been initially uneasy about going to Paxton's alone, Matt and his two friends had invited her to join them at their table, which had helped to calm her nerves. They'd been polite and fun and she'd enjoyed dancing and conversing with them, but there had been no sparks or real chemistry. How could there be when she'd compared each one to Cole and found them lacking in some way?

She couldn't say she was completely surprised to find out that Cole had followed her to Paxton's. She'd even been pleased by his appearance, since his presence had allowed her to feel a bit more secure and at ease. It was his boorish, take-charge attitude that had rubbed her raw and instigated a flare of rebellion.

Despite still being mad at him, a small smile touched her lips as she recalled their naughty escapade out on the dance floor. For those few precious moments he'd been hers, with nothing between them but desire and pleasure. That tryst had been one of the most erotic, thrilling experiences of her life, and she'd basked in her body's instantaneous and effortless response to Cole—until he'd abruptly decided that it was time he took her home.

Hurt and confusion had prompted her to defy him by any means available, which accounted for her reluctance to leave the club with him. It was beyond her comprehension how Cole could make her body burn for him one minute, then withdraw in the next, shutting her out physically and emotionally. Even now her nerves still thrummed for something more, and there he sat across from her, impenetrable as stone.

She wondered what it would take to truly crack that resolute demeanor of his, to completely unleash the intensely sexual man she'd seen glimpses of in the past week. The thought fascinated and excited her, and caused a flush of intrigue to sweep across her skin. But then reality intruded and reminded her how carefully Cole guarded his responses to her.

The vehicle came to a smooth stop and Cole cut the engine. Melodie frowned as her surroundings came into focus and she realized they were parked in his driveway.

"What are we doing here?" she demanded.

"You're staying at my place for the night." He withdrew the key from the ignition and turned to face her, his chiseled features illuminated by the streetlamp outside. "I want to be sure you don't do anything careless while you're still intoxicated."

Frustration welled up in her. "I'm not drunk," she insisted for the umpteenth time, then sighed, knowing he still didn't believe her. She was wasting her breath trying to convince him. "My shoulders and arms are killing me in this awkward position. Uncuff me, Cole." He hesitated long enough to ignite her temper all over again. "Oh, for God's sakes! I don't need to be restrained."

He lifted a dark brow, silently mocking her. "You know, I remember a time when you were sweet and accommodating and I never would have had to cuff you. Now you've turned into a hellion and I have no idea what you're going to do next."

Being passive had gotten her nowhere, and she liked her newfound femininity and the confidence that came with it. Even if Cole didn't. "What are you going to do, cuff me to your bed for the night to make sure I don't go anywhere?" The words slipped out of their own accord, and what was meant to be a sarcastic comment took on a very sexual connotation.

His eyes smoldered with heat and a breathtaking awareness. "Don't tempt me," he said, his tone low and rough.

A delicious pressure tightened in her belly as images of being at his mercy flitted through her mind. *As if that would ever happen!* Knowing Cole and that honorable streak of his, he'd shackle her to his bed and leave her there, alone, until morning.

"Take the cuffs off, *please?*" she said, giving him sweet and accommodating to get what *she* wanted.

Stretching across the console, he unlocked the metal bracelets, freeing her. "Behave yourself."

She rubbed her chafed wrists. "Thank you," she said curtly. Opening her door, she stepped out of the vehicle and headed for the street, not his house.

He scrambled from the car, his curses echoing in the night. "Where do you think you're going?" he called after her.

She didn't bother looking back. "Home, where you should have taken me."

Before she could retrieve her cell phone from her purse to call a cab, Cole was standing in front of her, his face reflecting impatience and something much more dangerous. She opened her mouth, intending to tell him to go away, but the words never had a fair chance to form as he bent low, jammed his broad shoulder into her midsection, and hefted her up and over his back like a sack of grain.

Her breath escaped in a sharp whoosh as she flipped upside down, arms flailing and her bottom sticking up in the air. Blood rushed to her head, making her dizzy, and it took her a few seconds to regain her bearings enough to express her indignation.

Gripping handfuls of his shirt, she braced her fists on his backside and tried twisting her body around to look at him, but only managed to cause a crick in her neck. "What do you think you're doing?"

His arm locked tight around the back of her knees to hold her in place as his stride quickened, jarring her with each step he took. "I'm taking you inside."

She could feel the muscles along his shoulders and back shifting, rippling, bunching as he moved, and the warm, masculine scent of him filled every breath she took, intoxicating her. "You can't keep manhandling me this way!"

"I wouldn't have to if you'd do as I say," he said rationally.

Releasing a low, peeved growl, she squirmed and wriggled and kicked her legs, railing at him to put her down. Ignoring her demands, he slipped his arm lower around her calves and clamped his other hand on her bare upper thigh to keep her still. His callused fingers abraded her sensitive skin and she gasped as a bright flare of desire electrified her.

Seething at his audacity and the absurdity of the situation, she blurted out, "I ought to bite you!" And the first place she'd sink her teeth into was his buttocks, she decided.

"I'll bite back," he drawled, his thumb stroking up her thigh, which quivered at his intimate caress. "And I've got access to a whole lot of tender flesh, so you'd better think twice before doing something so rash."

Keys rattled as he unlocked his front door. Walking inside, he flipped on a light and started up the stairs to the second floor, mindless of the discomfort he was causing her.

She smacked him on the butt with her hand, and grimaced as her palm stung. Was there *anything* soft about his man? "Dammit, Cole, put me down!" she snapped, growing tired of his dominance. "I'm not your responsibility or obligation."

He snorted at that. "The way you were acting at Paxton's tonight, someone has to look after you."

"And you decided you're the best person to play guardian angel?" she asked incredulously.

"I've never claimed to be an angel," he told her, his deep voice vibrating with a subtle warning. "So don't push me because you won't like the consequences."

Her mouth fell open as a slow, steady steam of fury gathered inside of her. "Is that a *threat?*"

"It's a *promise.*" At the top of the stairs he turned to the right and headed down a short hallway with her still slung over his shoulder. "I'm not in the mood to deal with any more of your reckless antics."

"And I'm not in the mood to deal with your barbaric attitude," she shot right back. "This sucks, Cole!"

He tsk-tsked her as he entered a dark room. "Now you're getting a potty mouth, too."

She laughed, but there was no real humor in the sound. "What are you going to do? Wash my mouth out with soap?"

He snapped on a bedside lamp, illuminating the area, and she blinked as her eyes quickly adjusted to the light. From her upside-down position she took in dark, masculine furnishings and a huge four-poster bed. Finally, he set her back on her feet, and her purse fell to the floor. When she stumbled backward to gain her footing on the three-inch heels, he grabbed her arm before she ended up on her bottom alongside the purse.

Once she'd regained her equilibrium, he let her go. Sitting on the edge of the bed, he leveled her with an arrogant look, his dark, fiery eyes equally bold and direct. "I'm thinking I ought to take you over my knee and give you the spanking you deserve for your scandalous behavior."

A sinful thrill shot through her veins, settling in her belly like liquid heat. "Oh yeah?" she taunted, baiting him in a way that wasn't smart, but she no longer cared. "I dare you to even try!"

Before she could draw her next breath he snagged her wrist, tugged her to him, and she found herself draped over his lap, face down, with his strong thighs supporting her. One big hand cupped a soft, rounded cheek, squeezed as if testing the resiliency of her flesh, and her heartbeat tripled.

She swallowed hard. Oh, Lord, she'd pushed him too far, and he was going to give her exactly what she'd asked for. He was going to spank her.

7

KNOWING SHE DESERVED the punishment Cole was about to mete out for taunting him, Melodie's entire body tensed in anxious anticipation as she waited for the first smack to her bottom. Long, suspended moments passed, but instead of the stinging swat she'd prepared herself for, his splayed hand gently kneaded her buttocks and his thumb traced the crease in between. In their scuffle, her dress had ridden up, and his palm continued its downward exploration to her bare thighs.

Cole's breathing grew heavy, as if he were lost in a deep trance, his fierce erection pressing against her hip. She bit her bottom lip and shivered, afraid to say anything that might break the sensual spell cast over him, afraid he'd come to his senses and stop the exquisite pleasure of his touch.

The warm, blunt tips of his fingers feathered the inside of her trembling thighs, and her legs widened of their own accord, welcoming his caress. Bolder still, he slipped beneath the hem of her dress where he came into contact with the barrier of her panties. Following the panel of silk to her feminine mound, he encountered the warm, wet evidence of her arousal. Groaning deep in his throat at what he'd discovered, he rubbed the damp, slick fabric against her swollen, aching flesh and plied her clitoris with slow, circular strokes.

It seemed her climax at the club had only whet her appetite for more, because that easily, that quickly, another orgasm beckoned. Instinctively she arched her hips against his hand, her fingers biting into the taut muscles in his thighs where she braced herself. She trembled at the sensations washing over her, moaned at the heated pressure building inside her, needing more, needing *Cole*.

She twisted around to glance up at him. His features were etched with a searing hunger, his eyes feverish and hot. He wanted her, too, and that knowledge thrilled her. "Cole...*please*."

He blinked as if someone had slapped him, looking startled, the seductive moment shattered. "No," he grated in an agonized tone, then more firmly added, *"No,"* as if he had to convince himself to stop touching her.

He gave her a gentle push off his lap and she slid to her knees in front of him. "Cole?" she questioned, needing some kind of explanation for his withdrawal.

He closed his eyes and pinched the bridge of his nose between his fingers. His chest rose and fell as he took a deep, shaky breath and let it out. "This *can't* happen."

It was the same old argument, and tonight she wasn't going to let him dismiss their attraction without a fight. She pulled his hand away, forcing him to look at her. He did so with a familiar scowl that made her smile.

"It *can* happen, if you let it." Swallowing hard to calm her own nerves and racing heart, she eased his knees apart and moved in between so that his thighs bracketed her waist. "I've never wanted another man the way I want you, Cole."

Taking advantage of their provocative position, she reached for the waistband of his jeans and unfastened the top button. She gripped the tab of his zipper, but before she could ease it down and over the enormous erection straining the front of his pants, he caught her wrists, holding her at bay.

"Mel..."

"Don't tell me no, Cole," she said before he could express his own denial. "Not tonight."

Leaning into him, she placed an open-mouthed kiss on the taut material stretching across his groin. She rubbed her cheek against his heat, breathed in the musky, male scent of his arousal. "I want this and I want you."

"You're not thinking straight," he said hoarsely.

She lifted her head, shaking her tousled hair out of her face. "My mind is perfectly clear."

He laughed abruptly. "Not likely. You were drinking like a fish at the nightclub!"

Shrugging, she placed her hands on his chest, aching to touch his naked flesh. "I was thirsty."

The disbelief in his eyes was plain to see. "I won't take advantage of you when you've been drinking."

She sighed and brushed the tips of her fingers along his clenched jaw. "You're so noble, Cole, so damn honorable. While I admire those traits in a man, it's the last thing I want from you right now." She paused a moment, then added, "I was drinking ginger ale with lemon."

He frowned, and she knew he was about to debate the issue with her. So she proved her claim the only way she knew how. Curling a hand around the back of his neck, she pulled his mouth down to hers. Lips meshed, parted, and her tongue slid deep inside in a long, hot kiss as she let him taste and sample the lemon essence still lingering on her tongue.

She was the first to pull back, which she took as a positive sign. "See?" she said breathlessly as she dragged her hands down to his chest. His rapid heartbeat thumped wildly beneath her palm and she experienced a jolt of satisfaction knowing the kiss had excited him as much as it had her. "Not a drop of alcohol."

He stared at her, his stunned expression gradually ebbing to contrition. "I apologize for accusing you of being drunk," he said reluctantly, huskily.

Ah, hearing Cole admit that he was sorry was very sweet, indeed. "An honest mistake I can forgive," she replied with a slow, beguiling smile. "But just for future reference, don't make assumptions about me until you check out the facts."

He lifted a dark brow, a rare glimmer of amusement making an appearance in his eyes. "Are you attacking my credibility as a P.I.?"

"Just making sure you no longer automatically jump to conclusions as far as I'm concerned." Still on her knees before him, she held his gaze as her hands skimmed lower, over his taut belly, and was gratified when he didn't try and stop her slow caress this time. "And here's another fact for you, Cole Sommers. There's no way you can take advantage of me when I'm a willing participant."

He opened his mouth to reply, and she pressed her fingers over his lips, shaking her head. "No more excuses," she said quickly, unwilling to give him the opportunity to reject her. Yanking his shirt out of the waistband of his jeans, she worked it up and over his head, relieved when he lifted his arms to help her instead of putting up a struggle.

His resistance toward her seemed to be fading, and she seized the opportunity to secure his acquiescence. "I know you want this as much as I do. Maybe more," she added seductively, and trailed the tip of her finger down the elongated bulge hidden under the denim. Heat radiated off him, singeing her fingers. "Am I right?"

His gaze darkened like midnight, and his mouth twisted with a smile that reflected wry humor and unmistakable arousal. "How can I deny the obvious?" he rasped. "The evidence you've discovered speaks for itself."

And the proof of his desire was screaming to be released from confinement. Taking his comment for the permission she sought, and reveling in the power that was momentarily hers, she proceeded to carefully drag the zipper of his jeans down, anxious to free him to her avid gaze, her eager touch. Much to her surprise he didn't stop her when she pulled his briefs down and took the hard, throbbing length of his penis in her hand.

He sucked in a deep breath and his hips bucked as she stroked experimentally. Awed by the impressive size of him, spellbound by the hot, velvety texture of his rigid flesh, she slid her fingers lower and gently fondled his taut sacs. His eyes squeezed shut, his jaw locked, and she watched in fascination as the muscles in his abdomen flexed and rippled.

Sharp awareness and acute need flared in her belly like a ball of fire and spread through her bloodstream, eliciting a slick, erotic warmth between her thighs. She looked up at his face, flushed with aroused color, his gaze heavy-lidded with unbridled lust and a primal need she wanted to satisfy.

"I've...I've never done this before," she whispered. "Tell me what to do. Tell me what you like."

She'd never been so sexually aggressive and straightforward with a man, but there was so much at stake for her. More than just giving her body to Cole, her heart and emotions were involved as well, and she wasn't going to let this chance to know him so intimately slip through her grasp. And, luckily, he was willing to accommodate her request.

He brought her hand to his mouth and licked her palm and fingers, thoroughly dampening her skin. Wrapping her fingers around the hard base of his penis, he guided her hand slowly, firmly, up the length of his shaft, then down again.

He taught her exactly what he liked, told her with a low groan how much he enjoyed her slick touch. She picked up his rhythm quickly, completely enthralled at the way his erection pumped through her tight fist, pulsating, growing impossibly longer, harder, with each stroke.

His hand abandoned hers and he braced his palms on the mattress and leaned back, offering himself up to her. She blatantly looked her fill of his naked body, brushed her thumb over the smooth, broad tip of his shaft, and he shuddered in response.

Knowing she might never get another opportunity to indulge in her own personal fantasies, she raised up on her knees, shifted between his thighs, and skimmed her soft, seeking lips along his chest, scattering moist, open-mouthed kisses on his heated flesh. She found a taut nipple and licked, and he gave a rough sound of pleasure that encouraged her to explore farther. Working her way lower, she nibbled her way down to his abdomen, inhaling his incredible scent and relishing the saltiness of his skin.

She licked her bottom lip, the male flavor of him making her crave to taste him elsewhere. His entire body tensed when she lowered her head once more and daringly lapped her tongue over the head of his penis.

He trembled with restraint, and his noble resistance was the last thing she wanted from him. She met his gaze, her own body growing damp with gathering expectation. "Tell me what to do, Cole."

He gently touched the back of her head, pressing her closer. "Take me in your mouth," he said, his low voice tinged with a thread of desperation. "As much as you can."

She parted her lips and drew him in, using her tongue to stroke, lick and swirl along his length. His hands threaded through her hair, and his fingers massaged the back of her scalp, gently urging her to take more of him.

Wanting to experience everything he had to offer, she took him deeper. His hips moved in sinuous gyrations, and then she sucked, letting instincts and a wild need to devour him, all of him, drive her.

He groaned like a dying man, and long before she

was ready to quit he gently pulled her mouth away from him. His chest heaved as he gasped for breath, and she wasted no time in tugging his pants and briefs down his legs and tossing them aside. When he was magnificently naked she reached out to touch him again, but he quickly intercepted her move by grabbing her beneath the arms and hauling her up onto his big bed.

Sprawled in the middle of his comforter, she came up on her elbows and found him standing by the edge of the mattress by her feet, a possessive, primal look in his eyes that made her shiver with delight. "I'm feeling a bit overdressed."

He flashed a smile, as tempting as sin itself. "Don't worry, sweetheart. I plan to take care of that little problem."

Slipping a shoe off her foot, he ran the pad of his thumb down her sole, making her toes curl and a rumbling purr escape her throat. He repeated the process with her other foot, then crawled over her like a predatory jungle cat claiming his mate. Straddling her hips, he locked his knees against her waist. He was careful to keep his full weight off of her, but the decadent sensation of being pinned beneath him, a captive to any and every wicked predilection he might have, made her feel light-headed and sensually charged.

He bent over her, nuzzling her neck with his lips as his long, strong fingers slipped beneath the thin straps of her dress and slowly, gradually, pulled them down her arms, tormenting her every inch of the way. He kissed her exposed flesh, and her breath caught when his tongue dipped between her breasts then up and over the soft, aching swells straining at the bodice.

Unable to stand any more of his teasing, she placed her hands over his and tugged the dress lower, freeing her breasts to the cool air in the room. Her skin drew tight and goose bumps rose on her flesh. Trapping his face between her palms, she guided his lips to her nipple. He latched onto the hardened crest, his teeth scraping deliciously, his tongue swirling, his mouth tugging, pulling and suckling the engorged tip.

She writhed beneath him and cried out, and he continued to drive her steadily into that feverish realm where nothing existed but pleasure and hot, clawing need. Just when she felt as though she was about to come apart, he slid lower and proceeded to peel the clingy fabric from her body, his lips and soft tongue continuing a downward journey over her belly, around her navel, and along her hip, making her breathless with anticipation.

He stripped the dress from her body and hooked his thumbs beneath the elastic band of her underwear to render her completely bare. Struck by a moment of modesty, she grabbed his wrist to stop him. Once he removed her panties she'd be at her most vulnerable, with nowhere to hide her body's response to him.

His dark face wavered before her, his eyes hot and fierce, and she felt scorched by the intensity burning between them. "You started this," he murmured, his voice hoarse with passion and a need that equaled her own. "I want to taste you, too. All of you."

He easily could have shaken off her grasp and done as he pleased, yet he waited for her to make the decision to trust him. And she did, unconditionally. Knowing that, it was incredibly easy to release his hand, let him remove the last article of clothing between them, and allow him free access to her heart, body and soul.

Gently parting her legs, he rained hot kisses along her calves, tongued and suckled the sensitive spot behind her knees, and nibbled from thigh to thigh. The bites grew sensuous and lingering, his breath erratic and hot as he made his way closer to the most intimate part of her.

Her hips tilted in automatic reflex, and she moaned as a finger slipped inside her—long, hard and virile—slowly thrusting deep. A prelude of what was to come. She could feel her own wetness and she trembled when his thumb delved along her sex, followed by the heat of his breath, the languorous lick of his seeking tongue.

She bit her lower lip to hold back a scream, but

there was no prolonging the exquisite pressure building within her. She was too ready, too primed, and he already knew what it took to send her over the razor-sharp edge to a stunning orgasm. All she could do was grip the comforter in her fists and ride on the wave of the hot, explosive contractions pulsing through her.

Cole levered his strong, muscular body over hers, but didn't enter her as she expected him to. Instead, he feathered soft kisses across her eyelids, temples and jaw, seemingly sensing that she needed the comfort of his gentle touch in the aftermath of such an overwhelming climax. Her trembling eventually subsided, and Cole dropped his forehead to hers, heaving a long, drawn-out sigh.

"Damn," he muttered, and started to move off her.

Startled, she caught his arms and curled her calves over the back of his strong legs, refusing to let him go. "Cole, what's wrong?" They'd come so far, she wasn't going to let him retreat so easily.

"I'm sorry, Mel," he rasped, the disappointment in his gaze clear. "I don't have any condoms, and there's no way in hell I'd risk getting you pregnant."

Grateful for such a legitimate excuse, relief poured through her, and she smiled. "I have condoms."

He frowned. "Oh?"

"They're in my purse," she said, playfully skimming her fingers down his spine to his buttocks. "About half a dozen of them."

He looked horrified at the quantity she named, and she laughed, easily imagining what was going through that overly protective head of his—that she'd been on the prowl tonight at Paxton's for a man to have sex with.

"I was hoping to get lucky...with you," she added softly, making sure he knew that there was no one else she would have considered sleeping with. "And I wanted to be prepared."

His gaze bore into hers. "How did you know we'd make love?"

"I didn't. It was pure wishful thinking on my part. Well, maybe not so pure." She laughed and stroked the hair at the nape of his neck, loving the way the silky texture slid through her fingers, a direct contrast to the hard body poised above her. "And just in case you care, you're seriously killing the mood with your twenty questions," she teased.

He shook his head, a rare, genuine smile softening his features as he left her to retrieve the small purse on the floor. "We really are going to have to do something about that smart mouth of yours." Finding a handful of prophylactics, he set them on the nightstand by the bed and tore open one packet to use.

Stretching like a content cat, she watched as he sheathed himself, his movements precise and very sexy. "I'm sure you can find some way to keep this smart mouth of mine busy."

"Oh, yeah," he growled and moved back to the bed. He spread her thighs with his own as he eased over her and braced a forearm along the side of her head. Caressing his other hand down to her hip, he positioned her, holding her open for his possession.

Wasting no more time on foreplay, he sank into her with one hard, driving thrust. Despite being wet and ready for him, she sucked in a sharp breath and arched against his hips, overwhelmed by the uncompromising maleness stretching her, impaling her to the hilt, filling her like nothing ever had. Slick and hot and deep.

Cole stilled, the pulse beating in his throat tripling. "Oh, no," he breathed as he frantically searched her gaze. "Tell me you're not a virgin."

"I'm not," she reassured him, welcoming the few extra moments for her body to adjust to the breadth of him. "It's just been a while for me."

He brushed tendrils of hair off her cheek, his touch so tender, his gaze brimming with so much concern, her heart ached. "How long?"

"It was over three years ago with an old boyfriend." She shrugged, the incident an inconsequential one compared to being with Cole. "Besides, I don't think it's me so much as it's *you*."

He looked taken aback. "Excuse me?"

She smiled impishly. "You're much bigger than

what I've had before, not that I'm complaining. I'm getting used to the size of you real quick."

"Thank goodness, because you feel incredible, so warm and tight and I can't wait much longer..." He flexed his hips, forcing his way deeper, and groaned at the internal friction he caused.

Wanting him to lose that precious hold on his control, she raised her knees, wrapped her legs around the back of his thighs, and urged him to move.

His nostrils flared, his blue eyes blazed, and his legendary restraint finally snapped. He began sliding within her, lithe and strong, and there was nothing sweet, slow, or gentle about his possession. His body was on fire, and he fanned the flame with every stroke, taking her just as high.

He lowered his head and captured her mouth in a hungry, greedy, tongue-tangling kiss she returned just as voraciously. Her soft breasts crushed against his chest, and keen sensation curled in her loins from the undulating pressure against her femininity as he pumped faster, harder, a desperate urgency to his thrusts.

She writhed and arched and moaned, her passion as wild and untamed as his. The increasing tension surging through her stole her breath, and then she was coming, unraveling from the inside out, her inner muscles clenching in small spasms around his burgeoning shaft. He tossed his head back and, with a low, savage groan that vibrated its way up from his chest and one final, frenzied thrust, she felt his own release rip through him in powerful, endless waves of pleasure.

He collapsed on top of her, muscles quivering, and she held him close, heartbeat to heartbeat, while his hot, panting breath fanned her throat. She closed her eyes, savoring the moment, suspecting it would be over much too soon. Reality would eventually intrude, as would Cole's honorable, responsible streak.

Making love with Cole was everything she'd dreamed it would be, and she was all too aware of the fact that he hadn't made her any promises. Not that she expected any from a man who avoided emotional commitments with women and had tried to warn her many times not to get involved with him. Even knowing that he wasn't the type to let a woman tie him down, a troubling thought niggled the back of her mind.

Now that she'd had Cole Sommers, how was she ever going to give him up?

COLE WOKE UP the following morning alone in his bed. The covers next to him were rumpled, reminding him of how he'd spent the night, and with whom.

Oh, man.

He'd made love to Melodie. Not just once, not

twice, but three incredible times. Hell, he still wanted her if the erection he was sporting this morning was any indication.

The realization stunned him and brought on a whole slew of complications he wasn't prepared to deal with, such as what did she expect of him now that they'd crossed that line between friends and lovers? How would last night change their working relationship? And would Richard disown him if he ever discovered what he'd done with his daughter?

His gut twisted with uncertainties. He didn't have any ready answers to those questions—at least none that reassured him.

Releasing a deep exhale, he scrubbed a hand along the stubble on his jaw, unable to believe that he'd allowed his attraction to Melodie to overrule his common sense. Yet there was no denying that being with her had felt good and right, like everything that had been missing from his life—a gentleness, understanding and rare chemistry that blended sexual awareness with a sense of comfort and security.

Beyond physical pleasure, there had been an emotional connection between them unlike anything he'd ever experienced with another woman. There were intense, possessive feelings he'd always sworn he didn't need or want in his life because he'd seen with his mother and father how much heartache it could cause.

Reaching out, he touched the vacant spot next to him, a foreign disappointment settling deep. The sheets were cool, indicating that Melodie must have slipped out a while ago, and the only way she could have left was by cab, prompting him to recall the comment she'd made last night after the first time they'd made love. Very quietly and without any ulterior motives attached, she'd suggested that since she wasn't intoxicated as he'd originally assumed, he could take her back to Paxton's so she could pick up her car and go home.

Part of him had appreciated the offer, since he didn't make a habit of letting women stay the night because of all the expectations that came with such an intimate invitation. But he hadn't wanted to treat Melodie like a cheap one-night stand. And he'd honestly wanted her to stay. Convincing her that his offer was genuine had been ridiculously easy and just a matter of kissing her, touching her and making her body come alive for him again. She was easily distracted, very willing to try anything he suggested, and more adventurous in bed than he ever would have imagined.

He shook his head, still amazed that she hadn't pressured him for more than what he'd given her last night. There had been no after-sex expectations, and no smothering or emotional demands. She'd given him incredible, mind-blowing, guilt-free sex. So why did he feel so annoyed for waking up alone?

He sat up, intending to get out of bed, when a small piece of paper on the pillow next to his caught his attention. He picked up the note, recognized Melodie's handwriting, and knew she'd written another fantasy for him.

Last night you satisfied me with your touch, yet come the dawn, I want you just as much. I'll never get enough of you.

Your scent still lingers on my skin, arousing my desire, making me breathless for your caress. I'll never get enough of you.

Your passionate embrace started a fire in my soul, one that still burns bright and hot. I'll never get enough of you.

The letter was short, simple, and so very evocative, affecting him on a gut-deep level. He swallowed the lump in his throat and stilled the rapid beat of his heart, refusing to delve too deeply into the message behind her words. Unfortunately, there was nothing he could do to dismiss the echo of her declaration. *I'll never get enough of you.*

The sound of soft footsteps padding up his stairs startled him and made him frown, especially since he'd thought he was alone. Setting the erotic letter on the nightstand, he sat up straighter and yanked the sheet over his lap and stiff erection. Seconds later, Melodie walked into his room with two mugs of steaming coffee in her hands and a sweet, dreamy smile on her lips.

Instead of the scrap of a dress she'd worn last night, she'd donned one of his button-up shirts from his closet, leaving her long, slender legs gloriously bare. Her hair was tousled around her head, her lips were red and puffy from their ardent kisses, and there were a few faint love bites on her neck that he'd given her in the throes of passion.

But what captured his attention the most was her face. She'd washed her skin free of the makeup she'd worn last night, giving her a girl-next-door kind of look that was soft and pretty and unassuming. While he had to admit her sexy persona was exciting as hell, she was a woman who truly didn't need any artificial enhancements to attract a man. Her skin positively glowed, as did her deep brown eyes.

"Good morning," she said shyly, and handed him one of the mugs of coffee, made with cream just the way he preferred.

Taking the hot drink, and still shocked by her presence, he blurted, "You're still here."

Her eyes widened with sudden uncertainty and she took a small step back. "You insisted that I stay last night," she said, her tone and body language reserved. "But I can go anytime."

He mentally kicked himself for handling the situation so poorly. "I'm sorry, I didn't mean to sound so crass. I woke up alone and I assumed you'd left."

A small, tentative smile curled the corner of her mouth. "There you go, making assumptions again."

"I'm afraid it's a bad habit I'm going to have to learn to break." Propping pillows against the headboard to lean against and keeping the covers pulled to his waist, he patted the mattress next to him. "Sit down and enjoy your coffee with me."

She climbed up on the bed and sat with her legs crossed. Taking a sip of her coffee, she studied him over the rim of her mug, then spoke. "I hope you're not berating yourself for last night."

He winced, wondering how in the hell she could read him so well. It was an unnerving feeling since he usually kept his emotions under lock and key. "About last night..."

She cut him off with a wave of her hand. "Don't you dare tell me it was a mistake, or you regret what happened." Her tone was light and playful, yet her soulful gaze told another story, that last night had been more than a frivolous tryst for her.

He sighed. No, he harbored no regrets, and that bothered him when he knew he ought to feel some kind of remorse for sleeping with her. "It won't happen again," he said softly.

A brown brow arched delicately. "You sure about that?"

He didn't miss the subtle dare in her question,

and it almost made him smile. He wasn't sure about anything anymore when it came to her, but he was going to do his damnedest to live up to this pledge. Keeping her at arm's length was more to her benefit than his own, and she'd thank him later for doing the right thing.

"There is something I need to talk to you about before I go," she said, drawing his gaze back to hers.

Cole braced himself. *Here we go*, he thought, suspecting they were about to embark on the dreaded morning-after conversation of how last night had changed things between them and where their relationship was headed now that they'd become lovers. The discussion was inevitable and something he wouldn't avoid talking about if it meant Melodie left with a better understanding of where things stood between them.

"What's on your mind?" he asked casually.

She took another drink of her coffee, then set the mug on the nightstand behind her. The movement caused the front of the shirt she wore to gape open, revealing the creamy slope of one breast. His mouth watered for a taste and his body throbbed with renewed desire. That quick, he ached to pull her beneath his hard body and bury himself in her soft, womanly warmth.

She folded her hands in her lap, her expression serious. "I want to work on the Russell case with you and attend the charity event next week as your date."

His mouth opened, then snapped shut again, her statement leaving him dumbfounded. He'd been prepared to divert a heartfelt spiel about how right they were for each other, not another campaign to convince him to let her accompany him to Thornton's mansion to read Elena's love letters.

Then a disturbing thought occurred to him. "Did you sleep with me in hopes that I'd change my mind about you working on the case with me?"

She leveled her gaze at him. "I slept with you because you're a very sexy man that I'm attracted to, and I know better than to think that sex would sway you into changing your mind about *anything*," she said wryly. "But I do think I've proven in many ways that I can handle the job. I'm familiar with the case, I'm capable of acting the part of your date, and you've seen for yourself that I can read an erotic love letter."

She wrote them damn well, too, he thought.

"So, since you've yet to hire anyone for the job after interviewing at least a half-dozen women with more silicone than brains, I'm asking for you to give *me* a chance."

He chuckled at her apt description of the women Noah had sent his way, and couldn't disagree with her point. "Why do you want this so badly?"

"Because I like the excitement of the business. I always have, and I want to be in a more active role for the agency. And then there's the fact that I'm discovering that I like stepping over the line of decorum every once in a while."

She tucked a stray strand of hair behind her ear, the artless gesture stirring his senses. "Being sensible and practical has its time and place, but being adventurous has definitely made my life more interesting."

And it was wreaking havoc with his. "I've already warned you that it could be dangerous," he said, and finished off his coffee. "If we're caught, Thornton would have every right to press charges and we'd most likely spend the night in jail and be slapped with a lawsuit. And if any of that happened, your father would never forgive me."

She reached for his empty cup and set it next to hers, then stretched out on her side next to him. "Why don't you let *me* worry about my father?"

He eyed where his shirt rode up on her thighs and wondered if she was wearing any panties beneath, then shook the thought from his head before he gave into the urge to check for himself. "Because your father trusts me to look after you and he doesn't want you getting hurt in any way. And if something happened to you, I'd feel responsible."

She sighed, the sound laced with impatience. "I'm absolving you of all responsibility when it comes to me, Cole, and I'd be happy to tell my father that, too, if it would help ease your conscience."

"No!" he said so abruptly that she actually flinched at his rough tone. Clearing his throat, he quickly gained his composure and softened his voice. "I mean, let's leave your father out of this."

"Exactly," she said smugly as her fingers toyed with the sheet draped over his lap, teasing him with her flirtatious behavior. "Let me accompany you to Thornton's, and it'll be our little secret that I'm working on the case." She winked playfully at him.

He narrowed his gaze, but his attempt at sternness was betrayed by the smile tugging at the corner of his mouth. "Why do I get the feeling that you're trying to blackmail me?"

"There's no blackmail involved. I've worked hard for you and the agency these past two years and I deserve this chance." She shrugged a shoulder. "Consider it a promotion if you like. I'm also perfect for the job, and I think you know it, too, or else you would have hired another woman by now."

She was so matter-of-fact that he could only stare at her and wonder if she was right. Had he subconsciously found fault with all those other applicants because once she'd made the suggestion to accompany him to the charity event no one else compared?

"What do you say, Cole?" she prompted, her eyes dancing with hope and a fresh eagerness he couldn't bring himself to dash. "I swear I won't disappoint you."

He knew that to be true. She was well qualified for the job. She'd issued a very convincing argument, one he could no longer realistically refute. "Fine, you've got the job."

She squealed with unfettered glee and leapt on top of him, hugging him tight. "Thank you, thank you, thank you!"

His body immediately responded to her enthusiastic embrace, hardening in a single rush of heat and desire. Her soft breasts felt like heaven against his chest, and he resented the thin sheet that separated his naked lower body from her soft thighs. Forgetting his vow not to touch her, he smoothed a hand down her back and over her hip. But before he could slip his fingers beneath his shirt to find out if she was naked, too, she lifted up on her hands and met his gaze, shattering the sensual moment.

"I promise you won't regret your decision," she said, grinning down at him.

The adoring look in her eyes made his pulse race. "Just remember that I'm in charge and you do as I say, no questions asked."

"I swear I will." She kissed him chastely on the cheek, her face wreathed with triumphant happiness.

In the next instant she moved off him and the bed, leaving nothing but cool air washing over his heated flesh. Scooping up her clothes from the floor, she headed for his bathroom, saying over her shoulder, "I'll get dressed and you can take me to get my car. I'm sure you have plenty to do today and I don't want to get in your way."

No, he really didn't have any plans, just work that he could easily put off until Monday. As she closed the door behind her and he sat alone in his bedroom with a raging hard-on with no relief in sight, he had the oddest feeling that he'd just experienced his first brush-off.

He rolled his shoulders and stacked his hands behind his head, confused and baffled by all that had just transpired in the past half hour.

There had been no talk of a relationship, and no mention of the tempting letter she'd written that stated she'd never get enough of him. It was as though last night and the fantastic sex they'd shared had never happened at all.

She was getting under his skin and throwing him off balance, and he had no idea what to expect from her anymore. She'd become an enigma, unpredictable and spontaneous, a woman full of sensual secrets that drew him. Seduced him. Thrilled him.

And now that he'd made love to her, he had no idea how he was going to resist her allure.

8

"HOW IN THE WORLD did you manage to convince my brother to let you accompany him on the Russell case?" Joelle asked Melodie, her amused voice drifting over the partition separating the boutique's dressing room from the viewing area.

"It was all a matter of showing him I was the right woman for the job," Melodie replied as she hung the four dresses she'd selected on the hook next to the mirror in her small cubicle. The charity auction was three days away, and she still needed an outfit for the black-tie affair. "And I do have to say, it's been fun doing so."

"I just bet!" Jo chuckled, the sound laced with mirth. "I have to give you credit, Mel. He's a hard man to convince when he's got his mind set on something, but he'd have to be half-dead if he didn't see all the changes in you over the past week and a half."

Cole had seen plenty, Melodie thought as she stepped into a slinky, glittery sheath. More than his sister or anyone else realized. He'd seen her naked, flushed with passion for him and writhing with desire beneath his hard, strong body. He'd seen her at her most uninhibited, and her most vulnerable. She'd shared nuances of her personality with Cole no other man had ever glimpsed before.

While he was familiar with the reliable, efficient secretary he'd hired, he was gradually discovering facets of the new woman she'd become. And she was fairly confident that he liked the fascinating combination, though a part of her couldn't help but wonder, when the case was over and there was no need to be quite so flashy to get his attention, would he still be so intrigued by her? Or was he only drawn to the bold, daring creature she'd recently become?

Day by day she was distinguishing what she liked best about the changes she'd made to her appearance and what she didn't care for. She loved certain aspects of being a sensual woman with naughty inclinations, but ultimately wanted to be true to her inner self and be comfortable in her own skin. And that meant tossing out her wilder, brazen antics and finding a balance somewhere in between.

Melodie straightened the dress over her figure, not caring for the way the metallic material scratched her skin when she moved. She preferred soft, silky material against her flesh, a recent luxury she'd come to enjoy with the lingerie she'd bought and the clothes she'd chosen to wear. The more sensuous fabrics reminded her of the way Cole's lips felt skimming along her belly and thighs. The smooth, sleek friction of satin and silk aroused her senses and kept her body and mind in touch with her newfound sensuality.

Even now, heat flowed through her veins and her nipples were taut and tingling, aching for Cole's touch to soothe the restless hunger that had grown over the past few days.

"The black sheath doesn't work for me," she called out to Jo, who was waiting for her to model the dresses for her. "I'm going to try on the next outfit."

"Okay," Jo said around a yawn. "Take your time. This chair is real comfy and I haven't had my afternoon nap yet."

Melodie laughed, shaking her head. "I swear, that baby has given you the best excuses to eat and sleep."

"I'm storing up on the sleep. From what everyone is telling me, I won't be getting much rest after the baby arrives."

Letting Jo relax for a few more minutes, Melodie stripped out of the first gown and put on the second, a lace slip dress that puckered in all the wrong places but did amazing things for her cleavage. She trailed her fingertips over the swell of her breasts and closed her eyes, imagining that Cole was in the cubicle with her, wishing it were his hands stroking her sensitive skin instead of her own.

It had been five days since they'd made love, and neither she nor Cole had brought up the erotic, unforgettable night they'd spent together, though the sexual tension between them at the office was at an all-time high...just as she'd intended, she mused with a secretive smile curving her lips.

Remembering an excerpt from *The Good Girl's Guide to Being Bad* about how men wanted what they couldn't easily have, Melodie had put the advice to good use the morning after they'd made love. Since she'd shown him how good it could be between them physically and emotionally, she'd decided she was then going to let those actions speak for themselves. Without pressure or smothering demands, she was giving Cole time and space to adjust to the change in their relationship, and though at times he still seemed confused by the change in her behavior, her strategy of being friendly and playful seemed to be working.

It had been difficult to resist opportunities to kiss Cole, but she'd managed to refrain and the anticipation between them had only increased. She'd allowed no touching beyond casual caresses and accidental brushes, but had indulged in a whole lot of teasing and long, lingering, seductive looks that seemed to keep him in a high state of awareness where she was concerned.

She'd been extremely careful not to give him any reason to throw up barriers or withdraw from her.

As a result of the playful friendship she'd established with him at the office, they'd formed a tentative, fragile bond. She felt optimistic that they might be able to work past Cole's reservations toward her and, in time, give an intimate relationship between them a chance.

Changing into the third garment, a bandeau-style dress, she stepped from the room to get Jo's opinion. "What do you think?" she asked, twirling for her friend's inspection.

"Hmmm. I can't say I love it," Jo said candidly, rubbing a spot on her belly where the baby seemed to be kicking a lot lately. "I think you could find something much more flattering."

Jo's honesty was the reason Melodie had brought her along to find an appropriate dress. She'd never had a mother or sister to give her advice, and she valued Jo's judgment.

"I can't say that it screams 'buy me' either," Melodie agreed, and flicked her finger at the bulky silk corsage sewn onto the waist of the gown. "I think it's this gaudy flower that makes me think of a prom dress."

"I think you're right," Jo said, grinning.

Returning to the changing room, she put the bandeau dress into the "no" pile, then turned to the final gown hanging on the hook. She'd saved her favorite choice for last, and she hoped it fit her.

"What's been going on with the Russell case anyway?" Jo asked from the other room. "I've seen Elena in the office a few times this past week."

Melodie took off her bra, since the dress was completely backless. "She's been briefing us on the layout of the mansion and giving us details of where and how to find the box of letters she needs me to read."

"Must be some pretty hot stuff they wrote to one another if Elena won't let Cole read them."

Removing the fancy black velvet halter dress from the hanger, Melodie carefully slipped the gown over her head before replying to Jo's comment. "I'm sure she feels the letters are too personal and private to share with just anyone."

Melodie could easily understand Elena's special request that a woman read the correspondence between her and her lover. Melodie's own letters to Cole were very intimate and provocative, written from her heart and soul, for his eyes only, and she'd be very reluctant to let anyone but Cole read them.

With a shimmy of her hips, the velvet fabric fell into place. The beaded halter top molded to her breasts and the tailored skirt draped perfectly along her waist as if it had been custom-made for her. The hem grazed her ankles, and there was a sexy slit in the leg that flashed a good amount of thigh when she walked. Striking a sultry pose, she held her hair up on the top of her head and let a few tendrils curl around her face and neck, completing the sophisticated look.

Oh, yeah, this dress was *the one*.

She bit her bottom lip and stared at her reflection, and while she was still amazed at her own transformation, she came to a stunning realization. Despite the outwardly conservative appearance she'd grown up with, she'd always been a seductive, sensual woman inside. It had just taken the right man to unleash all the daring, wanton impulses lurking just beneath the surface of her good-girl facade.

And no matter what ultimately happened between her and Cole, she had him to thank for giving her the courage to be such a confident, independent woman.

COLE'S GAZE kept returning to the smooth, bare expanse of Melodie's back as they mingled in the crowd of people attending the charity auction at Thornton's mansion. Something was different about the way she looked tonight, but he was having a heck of a time putting his finger on what it was.

When he'd arrived at her place a few hours ago to pick her up, he'd been bowled over by the woman who'd answered the door. She looked gorgeous and mouthwateringly sexy in her black velvet gown with the thigh-high slit, and her hair swept up onto the crown of her head, exposing the sensitive flesh at the back of her neck and the slender column of her throat. It was all he could do not to bend his head and sink his teeth into all that soft, pale flesh and mark her as his.

She was as sophisticated and beautiful as a woman could be, as well as charming and sweet to the guests they struck up conversations with during the cocktail hour and dinner. Her intelligence made her even more attractive, and her light laughter drew appreciative stares from many of the men in the ballroom. She was an overall perfect date, complementing him like no other woman ever had, and he felt damned lucky to have her on his arm.

He was also in a constant state of lust because of her. One week of spending time with Melodie and remaining celibate had made him feel sexually deprived and hornier than he could ever remember being. Arousal hummed just beneath the surface of his skin and his mind had a bad habit of conjuring fantasies of Melodie at the most inopportune times that left him hard and aching.

Now that he knew how good she felt beneath him, surrounding him, he wanted more of the same, and while she seemed completely uninfluenced by her hormones, his were on the verge of raging out of control. He feared it wouldn't take much at all for him to finally give into the excruciating, undeniable need to make love to her again, even though he knew he shouldn't.

The emcee for the night's festivities announced

that the charity auction would begin in ten minutes, and Melodie turned to him with a seductive smile. "Care to dance before the auction starts?"

Remembering what had transpired on the last dance floor they'd shared, a slow, drugging heat spread through his limbs. "Are you going to behave this time?"

She fluttered her long lashes innocently at him, contradicting the shameless glimmer in her eyes. "Do you really expect me to make such a promise and keep it?"

Her teasing, flirtatious response quickened his pulse, as she'd no doubt intended, and he didn't fight the sensation. Instead, he let her lead him into the midst of people enjoying the mellow tune the band played. He watched the sashay of her hips as she walked and thought about all that bare skin on her back he'd get to caress once he drew her into his embrace.

An overwhelming sense of déjà vu washed over him, and it finally clicked in his brain what was missing that he hadn't been able to pinpoint earlier.

Pulling her into his arms, he flattened his hand on her lower back and gathered her close, relishing the feel of her soft curves aligned against his body. He looked down at her smiling face and did his best to ignore the soft, parted lips begging for him to kiss. "What happened to the butterfly tattoo you had on your shoulder?"

She entwined her arms around his neck, crushing her unrestrained breasts against his chest. "It was one of those temporary tattoos you can buy in the store." She tipped her head, causing a wispy tendril of hair to brush along her cheek. "You didn't really think I'd get a *real* one, did you?"

Her tone was so incredulous that he winced, then laughed. "Well, yeah, I guess I did. Especially considering how impulsive you've been lately."

"It was fun to wear for a night, but I don't think I'll be getting a permanent one any time soon." Her fingers stroked the hair at the nape of his neck in a loving caress. "Did you like it?"

He couldn't lie. "It was very sexy."

A satisfied, feminine smile tugged at her mouth. "Just for your knowledge, I'm wearing another one tonight."

He groaned at the thought. "Not where I can see it, obviously."

A naughty sparkle lit her eyes. "No, not with the dress on," she confirmed.

His groin tightened and throbbed as he imagined stripping her bare to inspect all the places the tattoo could be hiding on her body...on her breasts, between her thighs, that sexy spot just at the base of her spine...

Clearing his throat, he steered his thoughts to tonight's business. "Are you ready to slip out of the ballroom when the auction starts?" he asked, his tone low so only she could hear.

She nodded. "As ready as I'll ever be."

He studied her expression as they swayed to the music gradually slowing to an end, searching for signs of worry or unease, but found none visible. "Are you nervous?" he asked, just to make sure he knew her frame of mind before they went any further.

"Not at all," she said with a realistic bout of confidence. "Actually, I feel energized. Do you ever feel that way when you're working undercover on a case?"

He grinned, very familiar with the rush of excitement coursing through her at the moment. "All the time." She was truly an amazing woman, and stronger and more competent than he ever would have given her credit for if she hadn't asserted herself.

The song came to an end, and as much as Cole enjoyed holding her in his arms, they had a job to do, a client's request to satisfy and Elena's reputation to salvage. The attendees gathered around the stage and podium set up for the auction, anxious to bid on jewelry, artwork and other collectibles, all for a good cause.

Jerry Thornton, a distinguished-looking man in his late fifties, took the microphone and formally welcomed everyone to the affair and went over the rules for bidding on a particular item.

"This is our cue to leave," Cole murmured, and casually ushered Melodie away from the crowd. In the pretense of searching for the bathroom, they headed down a nearby hall to the west wing of the house, as Elena had instructed. They nodded politely to the few people they passed along the way, until the voices from the ballroom grew dim and they came upon the staircase leading to the first floor of the mansion.

Ducking under the strip of tape blocking off the entrance to keep guests from straying, they quietly descended the stairs. Once they reached the bottom, they made a right turn down a wide corridor lined with an imported rug, counted to the third set of double doors on the left-hand side of the hallway, and slipped inside the room.

The smell of expensive tobacco and genuine leather assailed Cole's senses, and the moon filtering through the large window against the wall made the hardwood floor beneath their feet glow. Withdrawing the small flashlight he'd tucked into the pocket of his jacket, he switched it on so they could inspect the furnishings and the setup of the room.

The library was massive, with floor-to-ceiling built-in bookcases, a huge mahogany desk in the middle of the spacious room and a sitting area to the right with a large couch and two wing chairs facing a fireplace. Thornton most definitely had gobs of money, and he wasn't frugal about spending it, either.

"Elena said he kept the monogrammed leather box on the bottom shelf by the fireplace," Melodie whispered, and headed in that direction.

Cole followed, impressed by her sharp memory and her take-charge attitude. She was here to find a letter for a client, and she was solely focused on the job ahead. When they reached the bookcase, they crouched low and he flashed the beam of light across the lower shelves until they found the leather box Elena had given Thornton.

Melodie carefully pulled the monogrammed case from its cubbyhole and set it on the rug covering the hardwood floor. "That was ridiculously easy," she said, a thread of disappointment in her tone, as if she'd expected something more cloak-and-dagger.

Cole stifled a chuckle. "It's not as though Thornton was expecting anyone to come looking for the box, so he had no reason to hide it."

"Still, he should have been more cautious." Glancing over her shoulder at him, she held out her palm. "Hand me the flashlight so I can start reading the letters for you."

He did as she asked, unwilling to violate the terms of Elena's request by peeking over Melodie's shoulder, though he was sorely tempted. With her still kneeling on the floor near the fireplace, he moved to one of the wing chairs behind her, watching intently as she withdrew folded pieces of stationery, opened them up, and read the contents of each.

He kept an ear out for any sounds outside the library. All was quiet...except for the gradual deepening of Melodie's breathing as she scanned the provocative correspondences shared between two lovers. Her breasts rose and fell rapidly, and the glow of the flashlight wreathed her head in a soft halo of golden light and illuminated her profile and the pulse beating in her throat. Her lips were damp and parted, and she seemed mesmerized by the words, totally enthralled by the carnal fantasies Jerry and Elena had written for each other.

Cole shifted in his chair, feeling anxious and a little warm under the collar, and elsewhere. It seemed like hours had passed when it had only been a few minutes, but he had to do something to break the sexually charged silence in the room. "Did you find anything we can use yet?"

She wrenched her gaze away from a letter to look at him, her eyes glittering with the smoldering flame of passion. "No, not yet," she said, her voice soft and sensuous in the quiet room. "But I can see why she didn't want you to read these erotic letters. They're making *me* blush."

And aroused. He could hear the trembling desire

in her voice, see the carnal need in her expression, feel her growing anticipation. And like an animal drawn to the scent of his mate, he could smell her desire in the air, beckoning to him.

His chest heaved and his nostrils flared, and it was all he could do not to pounce on her and take her then and there on the floor. Hard and fast and deep. Lord knew he'd been ready and able all week, his body craving hers in a primal, elemental way that was slowly driving him mad.

She bent back to her task, and he glanced around the library, distracting himself by taking a visual inventory of all of Thornton's prized possessions.

"Here it is, Cole!" Melodie's voice rose in excitement, then quickly dropped when she realized the need for secrecy. "I found the letter."

He sat up straighter. "Are you sure it's the right letter, the one where Thornton tells Elena he's giving her the ring as a gift?" They only had one shot at this, and he didn't want to leave with the wrong correspondence.

"I'm positive." She shone the flashlight on the piece of paper and the bold, masculine writing filling the page. "It says right here at the end of all the risqué stuff, 'With this ring, I pledge to you my undying devotion. A gift from my heart to yours, an eternal reminder of the love we share. This ring is yours always, as is my heart, body and soul. Love, Jerry.'"

"That's it," he said, and came down to the floor to help her rearrange the letters she'd taken out of the box. "Put that letter in your purse and let's get everything back where we found it so we can get the hell out of here."

She stuffed the folded piece of stationery into her small velvet purse, then helped him clean up. Mission accomplished, they stood, and took two steps across the sitting area when Cole heard voices drifting from down the corridor, growing louder with each passing second.

"Shit," he muttered, and did the first thing that came to mind to save him and Melodie from being caught.

Dropping down onto the leather couch facing the fireplace, he pulled her on top of him so their feet were off the floor and she was secured tightly against him. He bent his knees to keep his shoes from hanging over the side of the sofa, and scooted his head down, hiding them from anyone who might walk through the door. His heart thundered in his chest, and Melodie stared down at him with wide eyes that reflected startled surprise.

"Don't move a muscle or say a word!" he ordered gruffly, and tucked her face against his neck to keep her quiet and still.

Seconds later a dim light switched on in the room and two male voices filled the silent library, their footsteps echoing on the polished hardwood floors as they made their way somewhere on the other side of the couch.

"I've got Churchills or Palma Larga," one man said. Cole recognized the voice as Thornton's, and they were talking about cigars. "What's your pleasure, Randall?"

Melodie's warm mouth fastened on Cole's neck, and the soft, unexpected stroke of her tongue made him tense and his breath suspend in his lungs. What in the hell was she doing?

"I'll take one of the Churchills," the other man replied.

"Good choice," Thornton said jovially.

Melodie continued tormenting him, stringing damp, quiet kisses up to his ear, then suckling on the lobe and grazing that sensitive bit of flesh with her teeth. Despite the very real threat of being caught, his body surged with a frenzy of wild need. What she was doing to him was shocking, and dangerous, and deliciously exciting. And there was no way to stop her without bringing attention to their presence.

And she had to realize that, as well.

The sound of Thornton opening a humidor could be heard, along with the rustle of him withdrawing the cigar the other man had chosen. "And I've got brandy upstairs and a poker game awaiting us once the guests leave in about an hour or so."

"You do throw the best parties, Thornton," the other man complimented.

"So I've been told." Thornton laughed. "Let's go enjoy these out on the upstairs terrace until the auction is over."

As the men headed back toward the door, Melodie dipped her tongue into the shell of Cole's ear. He swallowed a deep groan, squeezed his eyes shut, and tightened his fingers in her upswept hair. She was obviously feeling amorous after reading all those erotic letters, and once they were alone she was going to pay, and good, he decided.

The light switched off, throwing the library back into silent darkness, and the door clicked shut behind the men. Cole waited until the their voices faded away before he rasped, "What do you think you're doing, Mel?"

She moved sinuously on top of him, her breath hot and moist against his neck. *"I'll never get enough of you,"* she whispered huskily in his ear, the illicit words straight from the fantasy she'd left on his pillow last weekend.

Bracing her hands next to his head, she lifted her face from the crook of his neck and looked down at him, her expression all seductive sin in the moonlit library. "I need you, Cole." The raspy plea in her voice was unmistakable, reaching deep into his soul. "Right here, right now."

Oh, yes. He understood her need, because he'd

been fighting it all week, as well. He didn't hesitate, and he didn't question his actions or curse his lack of control as he'd done so many times since this craziness with Melodie had begun. He only knew that he couldn't refuse her, or himself, what they both wanted so badly. Right here, right now.

He sat up, taking her with him, positioning her so that she was straddling his thighs. He buried his fingers in her hair, sending a silver clip and pins scattering, and crushed his lips to hers. Filled with an explosive urgency, he took her mouth in a hungry, demanding, tongue-tangling kiss, the adrenaline rushing through his blood heightening the illicitness of their private tryst.

She made a soft, mewling sound in the back of her throat as her hands pushed aside his coat jacket and her fingers found the waistband of his slacks. She fumbled in her frantic haste to unbuckle the thin, black leather belt he wore, but she finally managed the deed, freeing his thick erection.

And then he was pulsing in her hands as she stroked him, squeezed him, making his entire body quiver from her practiced touch. He burned for her, desperate to be inside her. Sliding his hands into that tempting slit in her dress, he roughly yanked the velvety material up to her waist. Grabbing the elastic band of her black, lacy panties, he dragged them down her legs, and she stood up so he could completely remove the scrap of fabric.

He shoved the lingerie into his suit pocket for safekeeping, and she quickly pushed him back onto the couch, sliding eagerly back on top of him, spreading her legs on either side of his thighs. The broad tip of his penis slid against her damp, slick flesh, unerringly finding the opening to her body. Unable to wait any longer, he gripped her smooth bottom with both hands and thrust up and into her. She drew him in with a soft gasp of pleasure, flowing over him like liquid fire, hot and molten, consuming him.

A low, guttural groan escaped him at the snug, wet clasp of her body accepting him so completely. Closing her eyes, she tossed her head back and rocked against him, over him, her breath exhaling in soft, sensual pants. Her tempo increased as she rode him, and he pushed the heavy folds of her dress up to her waist and out of the way so he could watch her draw him deeper, clench him impossibly tighter.

And that's when he saw her tattoo in the moonlight—a small, impish fairy right above her feminine mound, the wings seemingly fluttering with every gyration of Melodie's hips. Fascinated, he brushed his thumb over the design then slipped his fingers lower, between her legs, caressing her where they joined so intimately.

Her orgasm hit hard and fast, the deep, rippling contractions triggering the beginning of his own climax. He pulled her mouth back to his and kissed her rapaciously, swallowing the sound of her wild, uninhibited cries as the overwhelming pressure built within him. His heartbeat thundered in his ears and he grasped her hips, lunging upward, hard and fast, again and again, penetrating deeper and deeper.

With a force that jerked them both, he poured himself into her, feeling his own scalding release coursing through him in powerful, endless spasms. His mind spun, and his chest tightened with a strange, intense emotion he couldn't ever remember experiencing before, a longing that shattered his defenses and shook him to the very core.

And then he knew, despite every effort to safeguard himself from this woman's allure, he'd fallen hard and deep for her. And the realization scared the hell out of him. But no more than the fact that they'd just engaged in unprotected sex.

9

"MELODIE, CAN I SEE YOU in my office, please?" Cole asked, his voice drifting through the intercom on her desk.

Cole's businesslike tone grated on her nerves and added to the growing frustration that had taken hold since Cole's immediate withdrawal from her after they'd made love in Thornton's library Saturday night. It was a normal response she should have grown used to, but she could have sworn the way he'd held her, kissed her and touched her had been different somehow. Obviously, she'd been wrong.

The Russell case was over and, apparently, so were they.

"I'll be right there," she said, equally careful to keep her tone impersonal as she finished typing up the final report for the Russell case to take in for Cole's signature.

Since that evening two nights ago, her emotions had run the gamut from confusion and dull misery, to familiar disappointment, to flat-out aggravation that he could so easily shut her out once again with no explanation. She'd done everything in her power to show him that what they shared went beyond a shameless seduction and hot, satisfying sex, but was rather a culmination of chemistry, caring and deep devotion. For both of them.

Not that he'd ever admit to needing her, or anyone else for that matter. For anything. And especially not for the kind of intimacy that meant exposing deeper layers of emotion and vulnerabilities. He was still struggling to keep her at arm's length, when it was the last thing she wanted or needed from him.

Determined to face him with her newly acquired confidence in place, she gathered the Russell file and headed into Cole's office. He sat behind his desk, shirtsleeves rolled up to his elbows, looking gorgeous and much too serious when she ached to see him smile at her, tease her, kiss her. It was as if their time together hadn't existed, and while she resented how effortlessly he could dismiss their affair, she refused to pressure him for more than he was willing to give her, no matter that her own heart was already his.

"Here's the final report and billing on the Russell case," she said, setting the paperwork on his desk in front of him. "Elena certainly seemed very pleased that we found the letter."

Cole nodded in agreement as he scrawled his signature across the final invoice, avoiding her gaze as he'd done all morning. "I'm sure the correspondence will go a long way in restoring her personal and professional reputation."

"For her sake, I hope so," she said, meaning it. She genuinely liked Elena and wished her the best. "But I do feel bad that things didn't work out for her and Jerry. There was a lot of passion between them in the letters they wrote to each other."

"Sometimes passion isn't enough to sustain a relationship," he said, thumbing through the paperwork in the Russell file to make a notation on one of the pages.

His matter-of-fact tone caused a sharp, twisting pain beneath her breast. He was talking about the two of them, she knew, and decided to throw out her own opinion on the matter. "No, I suppose not, but it's definitely a foundation on which to build a meaningful relationship. Passion can lead to love if the couple are willing to work at it."

Finally, he met her gaze, his vacant expression masking any emotions he might be feeling. "I guess that wasn't the case with Elena and Jerry."

And a relationship wasn't in their future, either, she read into his clever, double-edged statement. That easily, he'd completely severed the tentative, fragile bonds of the relationship they'd developed, shattering any last vestiges of hope she might have harbored and slapping her with a shocking dose of reality.

It was truly over between them.

She swallowed hard to keep her voice from betraying her internal pain. "You said you needed to see me for something?"

"A couple of things, actually." He waved a hand at the seat in front of his desk, his blue-eyed gaze briefly latching onto hers. "Sit down."

Too curious to find out what he had on his mind, she did as he requested.

A distant smile made an appearance. "I wanted to thank you for your help on the Russell case and give you this." He tossed an envelope across his desk for her to take. "You did a great job on Saturday night and I appreciate your professionalism."

Her professionalism? Dread swirled in her belly as she retrieved the envelope, opened it and pulled out a check for more than her normal monthly salary. Not knowing what to think anymore where Cole was concerned, her gaze shot to his. "What's this for?"

"A bonus for a job well done." He leaned back in his chair, the gesture putting even more physical and emotional distance between them. "You deserve it."

Fury welled up in her, but she kept a tight rein on her temper, resisting the impulse to smack Cole with the envelope clutched in her hand. She didn't want his gratitude or money for something that had been more than a job to her. She felt cheap and used and discarded, and wondered if this was Cole's way of assuaging his own guilt for giving into temptation and making love to her.

With her mind and stomach still reeling from the personal blow, she managed to choke out, "Thank you," and started to rise.

He stopped her before she could leave. "There's one other thing." He shifted uneasily, and a muscle in his jaw flexed. "We didn't use a condom Saturday night."

The switch in topic to more intimate matters startled her. The formal note to his voice and the way he was treating the entire incident like some kind of business transaction made her feel as cold as the money in her hand.

Their night of unprotected sex hadn't escaped her notice. Neither did the worried look currently etching Cole's features and darkening his eyes. After raising his brother and sister, he obviously wasn't eager to repeat the process with a family of his own. Not that she'd ever make those kinds of demands of him if he wasn't willing to give of his own accord. He'd made her no promises, and she would never use an unplanned pregnancy against a man to get what she wanted.

She wanted Cole out of love, not an obligation he felt bound to honor. And she didn't think he was capable of giving her the former.

She stared at him, unable to stop the hurt and anger that flowed through her, but she did her damnedest not to let him see her pain. "How about I let you know when I start my period?" she suggested.

He released a deep exhale that did nothing to ease the tension knotting across his stiff shoulders. "That would be great."

Pulling a sheaf of papers from a pile by his arm, he handed them her way, dismissing the topic that obviously made him feel very uncomfortable. "Here are the payables you needed me to approve for payment and a few statements that need to be filed."

Taking the paperwork, she left his office and returned to her desk. Despite her heartache, it was back to business as usual.

"Is EVERYTHING OKAY with you, honey?" Richard frowned at Melodie from across the restaurant table where they were having lunch together. "You don't seem quite yourself today."

Silently, she admitted to being more subdued and quiet than usual, mainly because she couldn't bring herself to be animated and cheerful when she'd spent a miserable week at work. She was slowly dying inside, while remaining outwardly indifferent to Cole's presence in order to get through each day. And, at night, all she had were heated memories to keep her company, and more written fantasies she'd penned for Cole that he would never read.

As for work, despite the professional job she'd done with Cole on the Russell case, it was obvious that she'd made no more headway with him in terms of being more than a secretary for Sommers Investigative Specialists.

"I'm good," she lied, and forced a smile that felt stiff on her lips. "I just have a lot on my mind."

"Oh?" Her father set his fork down on his plate and swiped his napkin across his mouth. "Anything I can help you sort out?"

She'd confided in her father many times over the years on different issues, and he always imparted good, solid advice she valued. But this time she couldn't bring herself to share the intimate details of her affair and breakup with Cole—for her sake as well as Cole's. "I think it's something that just has to work itself out on its own, if you know what I mean."

"Sure." He nodded in understanding, and reaching across the table, he settled his big, comforting hand over hers. "I hope you don't mind me saying this, but other than you being distracted, I'm glad to see that you're back to normal."

She laughed, the surge of humor a welcome release. "Back to normal? How do you mean?"

"Well, I admit to being worried by all the changes you've made recently, and while I think your haircut is great and I like the outfit you're wearing today, it just seems that you've settled down and mel-lowed back into my little girl. I suppose I have Cole to thank for that."

Cole? What did he have to do with anything? She frowned and pushed her plate aside, a niggle of unease fluttering in her belly. "What are you talking about, Dad?"

Richard clasped his hands on the table and ducked his head sheepishly. "I have to confess, I was concerned that the drastic change in your appearance was to get some man's attention, and my biggest fear was that whoever he was had taken advantage of you. So, I asked Cole to keep an eye on you, just to make sure everything was okay."

Melodie's lungs constricted, and it hurt to draw in a breath. Could her week get any worse?

She didn't want to believe what her father was telling her, but it made perfect sense and explained Cole's quest to safeguard her the past two weeks. He'd been doing her father a favor, owning up to yet another responsibility. Despite the times they'd made love, she'd ultimately been a duty for Cole, an obligation.

And she'd finally had enough from the well-meaning men in her life.

"You don't need to look after me, Dad, and neither does Cole," she said with more calm than she felt. She'd deal with her father now, and Cole later. "I've been on my own for years and I can take care of myself."

"I just can't help it," he said, his gaze imploring her to understand a father's concern. "I worry about you, and I knew I could trust Cole to make sure that you weren't getting into a situation you couldn't handle."

She could handle the situation just fine—it was Cole that was having a difficult time coming to grips with all the conflicting issues in his life that kept him from taking a few risks of his own. And she resented that she'd been caught in the middle of an arrangement between the two men she cared for the most.

"I love you, Dad, but I'm not your little girl anymore," she said, knowing the words needed to be spoken between father and daughter. "I know when Mom died you did your best to raise me and you were a great father in all the ways that mattered. I was so fortunate to have such a loving, caring dad who gave me the best of everything. But I'm a grown woman who needs her space to change and grow without feeling stifled, and that means no more trying to shelter or protect me. Let me make mistakes and learn from them."

"You're right," he replied gruffly, earnestly. "I guess it's just hard for me to let go of those parental instincts." He tipped his head and regarded her curiously. "Can I ask...did a man bring about all these changes with you?"

She wasn't going to lie, not when Cole had been such a huge part of her transformation into a stronger, more confident woman. "Yes, but it's over."

Compassion touched his features. "I'm sorry."

"Me, too. I'm certain you would have liked him." Smiling regretfully for what could have been, she got up from her seat, grabbed her purse, and came around the table to give her father a kiss on the cheek. "And now I need to get back to the office. There's some unfinished business there I have to take care of."

MELODIE CAME through Cole's office door without knocking, and the accusing look in her eyes put him on instant alert. Suspecting she had something other than business on her mind, he saved the Web site he was researching for a case and braced himself for the reason behind her abrupt interruption.

She marched up to the front of his desk, bold and fiery and so incredibly beautiful his heart thumped hard in his chest as it had done numerous times the past week. "Why didn't you tell me that my father asked you to look out for me like I'm some kind of child?" she demanded.

He winced at the underlying hurt in her tone and gave her the best answer he could, no matter how pitiful the excuse seemed, even to him. "Because I didn't think it was necessary to tell you."

"Or maybe it was because you couldn't bring yourself to say *no* to my father. You did the job you were asked to so you wouldn't disappoint him, despite *my* feelings on the matter," she said.

Her words hit, slamming into him hard. Mainly because she'd latched onto the truth he, himself, hadn't been able to face. Saying no to Richard hadn't been an option, not when the man had done so much for him since his own father's death, and not when he'd always given Cole his complete and utter trust in all things. Cole hadn't wanted to shatter Richard's faith in him, and that meant giving in to his appeal to watch over his daughter. But Cole also knew deep-down inside that even if Richard hadn't asked him to look out for Melodie, he would have taken it upon himself to do the deed, because it was in his nature to watch over and protect those he cared about.

And despite the way things had ended, Melodie was one of those people.

But that realization did nothing to change the situation as it currently stood—with Melodie reeling with a wealth of hurt and disillusionment and him berating himself for allowing his relationship with her to escalate beyond what either of them should have permitted.

"I'm sorry," he said, the words inadequate for all the misery and turmoil he'd caused—for both of them.

She hugged her arms over her chest, as if to hold herself together. "So, I was an obligation for you, a duty, like everything else in your life," she stated, her features reflecting her irritation.

His heart constricted in his chest, nearly suffocating him with remorse. Unable to sit still any longer, he stood and rounded the desk to where she stood. She took a step back, telling him without words that she didn't want to be touched.

"You were more than an obligation, Mel," he said, his voice rough, but undeniably truthful. "I'm at fault here, not you. I never, *ever*, should have touched you, not when I knew how things would eventually end."

She laughed cynically and shook her head. "Aren't you the honorable one." The comment sounded more like a curse than a compliment. "I'm surprised you're not insisting on marrying me because we had unprotected sex."

"If you're pregnant, you know I'll marry you," he replied automatically, defensively.

"Why? Because of my father? Because it's the right thing to do and you always own up to your responsibilities?" she asked, hitting upon another unpleasant nerve. "Thanks but no thanks. *If* I'm pregnant, I'll be a single mother who'll give you every right to be a part of your child's life. But I'm not about to marry a man who doesn't return my love."

Her words hit him like a sucker punch to his gut, and Cole inhaled a sharp, startled breath of air.

"That's right, I love you," she said softly. "But I'd

never trap you in a situation you'd come to resent. I know you had a rough childhood, and I admire you for being a strong, dedicated man despite your parents' divorce, and I think you're incredible for giving up years of your own life to raise your siblings after your father died. Even now, you continue to be the responsible one in your family, always in charge and solid as a rock. But have you ever stopped to think about yourself and what *you* might want for a change?"

He stiffened, annoyed that she somehow, someway, had the ability to dig past the surface and dissect the man beneath his controlled facade. "I have everything I could ever want." So why, then, did his bones ache at the thought of losing her? And why did his nights seem longer, lonelier, without her?

"Do you really?" Her beautiful brown eyes searched his, looking deep, deep into his soul. "You're always so quick to see to everyone else's needs and be strong and reliable and protective, but who takes of you, Cole?"

He shoved the tips of his fingers into the front pockets of his jeans. "Who says I need to be taken care of?"

"We all need that comfort and security once in a while. Even you, whether you can bring yourself to admit it or not." Her voice sounded tired. Tired of fighting him. "All I want is to take care of you, and be your friend and lover. I never mentioned marriage and I've never asked you for a commitment, though I'd be lying if I said I didn't want more than an affair with you. But all that's a moot point now, isn't it?''

The thick knot in his throat prevented him from answering her question, though his drawn-out silence spoke for itself.

She sighed heavily in defeat, then her chin raised a few notches, displaying a unique blend of gutsiness and vulnerability. ''The situation between us keeps getting worse, so I think it's best that I quit working for you.''

He blinked at her, one of his worst fears realized. ''You can't be serious,'' he barked.

Her eyes widened, then narrowed. ''And you can't be serious to think that I'd stay after everything that has happened between us, and how it's ended. I was really hoping that the Russell case would change your mind about me, not only as a lover, but as someone you respect in the business.''

A desperate, panicky sensation fisted inside him at the thought of her walking out that door, out of his life. And his tangled emotions had nothing to do with concern for her welfare and everything to do with a heart-wrenching fear he couldn't shake free. ''Mel—''

''You've already made your feelings perfectly clear, and so have I,'' she went on quickly. ''This is a choice I have to make for *me*. I want more than being a front-end secretary, but I don't see that happening because you'll never stop treating me as Richard's daughter, someone you have to look out for and protect. I need to go forward with my life, not remain stagnant, wishing and hoping for something that will never happen. So, I'm cutting my losses and moving on, with no regrets."

She was so proud, so fearless, so *courageous*—taking personal and emotional risks with her heart and accepting the outcome with grace, even though it wasn't in her favor.

"Tell me one thing before I go." Her voice quivered slightly, and her dark eyes glistened. "Were you ever attracted to *me*, or just the woman I created for the role in the Russell case?"

A long tension-filled moment passed between them. He was more than attracted, he'd fallen in love with her—the sensible, practical woman she'd been and the sexy, daring woman she'd become. But the words remained locked in his chest, because he knew he couldn't fulfill all the expectations that came with such a declaration.

"Never mind. Don't answer that," she said before he could summon a reply, the faint twist to her lips holding traces of resignation. "I don't think I want to know and possibly shatter my own personal illusions. It was a nice fantasy, while it lasted."

She turned and walked out of his office, leaving him cloaked in a thick silence and an awful, helpless emptiness he knew would consume him in the days, weeks and months to come.

"WHAT WOULD YOU SAY if I asked you to keep an eye on Melodie for me?" Cole asked his brother as they sat at a table at Murphy's one evening after work.

"I'd tell you to shove it," Noah replied, his tone laced with disgust. "I'm not about to tail her like she's some kind of parolee. If you want to know her daily agenda, then *you* follow her yourself." He shook his head. "God, you're pathetic."

Yeah, he was pathetic, and desperate, Cole silently admitted as he finished off his beer. He was equally chagrined with his obsessive need to keep tabs on Melodie, but couldn't seem to help himself, despite the difficult lesson he'd learned spying on Melodie for her father. "I just want to be sure she's doing okay."

"Who are you kidding?" Noah asked incredulously while signaling the bar waitress for a second round of drinks. "My guess is that you're trying to assuage your guilt for what happened between the two of you, which is ridiculous. Melodie's doing great. Better than you, anyway. According to Jo, she's out applying for jobs and has a few potential leads with other P.I. firms, while you've kept yourself holed up in your office. You're always distracted and grumpy, and you look like hell warmed over."

Natalie came by their table to deliver two more beers and a fresh bowl of peanuts, and while Noah paid for the drinks and flirted with the pretty bar waitress, Cole internalized his situation with Melodie until he felt as though he'd grown an ulcer.

Exhaling heavily, he scrubbed a hand along his taut jaw, the stubble on his face giving credence to his brother's remark about his unkempt appearance. Noah was right—he looked and felt like hell these days, like an intrinsic part of him was missing. He was floundering, trying to grasp onto any semblance of the control that had once come so easily to him.

Ever since he'd admitted to his attraction to Melodie, there had been no control over his heart or emotions. And because he'd chosen to mix business with pleasure, he'd lost the best damn secretary he'd ever had, which accounted in part for his feelings of disorientation at the office.

Yet he also acknowledged that he'd lost more than a secretary, and now that she was gone, he realized he'd depended on Melodie in ways that went beyond handling payables and receivables. She'd been someone he could bounce ideas off of, a trusted confidante, and she'd delved into cases with enthusiasm and interest, sometimes turning up information someone else had overlooked.

Nothing was the same without Melodie, and he couldn't bring himself to replace her. He'd lost much more than an efficient bookkeeper and assistant, he'd forfeited the warmth of friendship, the excitement and intimacy of a selfless lover. And he was certain no one could even come close to filling the void she'd left behind.

There were no more spontaneous lunches to enjoy, no smiles brightening his day, no erotic letters and no more shameless seductions. Many times he'd found himself heading out to the reception area to discuss a client with Melodie, or get an opinion on a case, only to remember that she was no longer there. No longer a part of his life. In any way.

There was no reason for him to contact her, especially since she'd left a message on his recorder at home a few nights ago reassuring him in an unemotional tone that she wasn't pregnant, after all. Instead of relief, he'd experienced an undefinable emotion that left him cold and empty inside.

Cole absently rubbed a spot on his chest, right where his heart beat heavily, achingly, as it had for the past week since the day Melodie had walked out of his office. He waited patiently for Natalie to move on to the next table, and noticed the way Noah's gaze followed the other woman in a slightly territorial way.

"Watch yourself with her," Cole said, feeling the need to dole out a bit of brotherly advice. "She doesn't seem like your love 'em and leave 'em type."

"Don't you worry about me," Noah drawled with a charming grin and tipped his bottle of beer Cole's way. "I know how to handle women, but you, on the other hand, have a whole lot to learn."

He couldn't bring himself to argue Noah's too-accurate statement. Cracking open the shell of a peanut, he tossed the nut into his mouth, chewed, then asked one of the questions that had been in the back of his mind for awhile now. "Do you ever think about what happened to Mom and Dad and feel as though their nasty divorce makes you more cautious about women and relationships?

Noah shrugged, not really answering the question for himself. "I think since you were the oldest, the divorce affected you the hardest, along with Dad's death. You've been so wrapped up in taking care of me and Jo for so long that you've never really had any time for you."

Cole shook off how Noah's words echoed his conversation with Melodie. "You both are grown and doing your own thing," he said, swiping his fingers down the condensation gathering on his beer glass. "I have plenty of time for me."

"And how do you spend that time?" Noah asked, and answered his own question before Cole did. "Working, at the office, at home, and having an occasional drink with a buddy. Don't you want more than that?"

Melodie had asked him the same thing. Until recently, he would have said no, that he was happy being a bachelor and was content with the way he lived his life. But his time with Melodie had changed his way of thinking and made him look at his life in a different way, made him wonder what he was missing out on because of his narrow-minded views on relationships.

Noah took a long swallow of his beer and eyed Cole candidly, brother to brother. "So, when are you going to face the fact that Melodie is the one for you?"

Cole raised a brow. "Excuse me?"

"I can see it and so can Jo," Noah went on ruthlessly. "Did you tell Melodie that you love her before she quit?"

Cole shifted under his brother's scrutiny. "What makes you think I love her?"

"Because I've never seen any woman tie you up in knots the way Mel has," Noah replied simply. "You're so in love with her you can't think straight." He held up a quick hand to stall Cole's automatic objection. "Don't bother denying it, because the only person you'll be fooling is yourself."

And fooling himself had gotten him nowhere, he realized.

Noah stood and picked up his bottle of beer. "Think about this mess you've made of things between you and Melodie, then do something about it before Jo and I strangle you."

Cole watched his brother head to the bar and take a seat at the end where Murphy put drinks for Natalie to deliver. Alone, Cole nursed his own beer and contemplated the situation until his head hurt. But no matter how many ways he viewed things, the conclusion was the same.

He loved Melodie and she was his life. He could choose to let her walk away or he could choose to win her back—for himself and for the agency.

The decision was his. A shiver rippled through him as everything clicked into place. Raising his siblings might not have been a choice for him, but a life with Melodie was.

Cole knew what he had to do. No more denying his feelings. No more excuses for keeping his distance. As for Richard, the older man would just have to accept that Cole was in love with his daughter.

He was going after Melodie—consequences be damned.

MELODIE WAS curled up in bed reading a romantic suspense novel, unable to sleep, when a loud knock sounded at her front door. She glanced at the clock on her nightstand and frowned. It was nearly eleven o'clock at night, and she'd never had anyone stop by so late. Her first thought was that the visitor was her father, but he wasn't the kind to drop by without calling first.

Feeling uneasy, yet curious to find out who was at her door, she set her book down, grabbed her old, favorite chenille robe and slipped into it as she headed down the hall. She looked out the peephole and saw no one, but was startled by the crinkle of paper beneath her bare toes.

Stepping back, she bent and cautiously picked up the cream-colored stationery that someone had shoved beneath the door. She instantly recognized Cole's handwriting. A tingling awareness pervaded her entire body, and her heart beat triple-time in her chest, echoing in her ears.

Swallowing hard, afraid to hope or assume anything, she read the words he'd written:

I never knew life could be so passionate and exciting until I fell for you. There's no denying the pleasure and ecstasy we shared. Now nothing will ever be the same. Take another chance on me.

There's nowhere else I'd rather be than with you. You're always in my thoughts, my dreams, and every fantasy I have revolves around this longing I have for you. I want to kiss you, hold you and love you. Take another chance on me.

I'm absolutely crazy about you. You're the only one for me, and I pledge on my honor to be forever true. If you're willing to take another chance on me, open the door and let me back into your life.

Giddy with indescribable emotions, Melodie hugged the fantasy close to her chest as Cole's words sank in, warm and wonderful and full of the kind of promises she'd ached to hear. She had resolved herself to the fact that they'd never come from the man who'd walked away from her, yet here he was, putting his own heart on the line, asking her to take another chance on him. On them.

Her answer came as naturally as breathing.

She opened the door, the gesture huge and significant for both of them. But welcoming Cole back into her life was so incredibly easy, because she not only loved him, she believed in him and his vow to her. In this case, his honor and integrity was a very good thing—it was that credible quality that made him a man she could trust with her heart.

He stood just beyond her threshold, his thick tousled hair and the stubble on his jaw darkening his eyes to a deeper, velvet shade of blue. A lopsided grin canted the corner of his mouth, but there was no mistaking the uncertainty etching his lean features.

"I'm not much of a poet," he said, looking like a young boy searching for her approval.

She resisted the urge to throw her arms around his neck and kiss him senseless, to reassure him with her touch that to her the words, written from his heart, were as eloquent as anything Shakespeare could have penned. "Your letter said all I needed to hear."

"Not quite," he said, his tone gruff. The invitation to enter her house had been issued the moment she'd opened the door, and he stepped inside, then turned to face her once again. "There's more I need to tell you."

She closed and locked the front door after him, then led the way into her living room. "Do I need to sit down for this?"

He smiled at her teasing tone and shook his head. "No, I think you can take it standing up. But you'll have to bear with me, because this relationship thing is all new to me and I'm sure I'm going to make a few mistakes along the way."

"I'll be here to help keep you on the straight and narrow," she said, and set his letter on the end table by the couch.

"I knew you would." He closed the distance between them and brushed the tips of his fingers along her cheek in a whisper of a caress that made her ache for more. "First of all, I'm not here out of obligation or a sense of duty. I'm here because I want to be."

She shivered as his finger absently trailed along her neck and followed the collar of her robe. "I never doubted that."

His gaze met hers, intent and determined. "And, secondly, I never did answer the question you asked me in my office—if I was ever attracted to the real you, or just the woman you'd created for the Russell case. I want you to know that I'm attracted to both the woman you were before you decided to make changes, and the woman you are now. Your intelligence and sweetness drew me in from the beginning and made me want you, and your new daring, confident attitude excites me. Despite the clothes, hair and outward changes, you've always been sexy to me."

Her breath caught and bubbles of exhilaration tickled her belly. But before she could respond, he continued on.

"There is absolutely nothing fake or pretentious about you. You're real and sincere, and you have the most uncanny ability to touch my emotions and make me *feel*. And, amazingly, you give of yourself and ask nothing of me in return, and that's something no one has ever done for me. You're truly more than I deserve, and while I'm scared of what you make me feel, because it's so intense, I can't let you go, either."

She bit her trembling bottom lip as renewed hope funneled through her. "I'll take whatever I can get from you, Cole. No pressure, no demands. Just take your time and we'll see where all this leads."

"For my sake, I'd appreciate it if we took things

slow and easy, but I don't need any more time to know and admit that I love you. All the time in the world won't change that fact."

Her eyes widened, her pulse sped up a few notches, and her knees went weak with disbelief. "You love me?"

"Oh, yeah, I do." His gaze devoured her, and in the twin depths she witnessed the truth of his heartfelt declaration. "I adore the way you laugh and smile and that sassy, seductive mouth of yours." Dipping his head, he nuzzled her neck and inhaled her scent. "I love the way you smell, the way you taste and how uninhibited you are with me." He settled a soft, lingering kiss on her lips and smiled down at her. "I pretty much love every single thing about you."

Tears stung the backs of her eyes, and she valiantly tried blinking them back. "I love you, too."

"I'm a damn lucky man." He framed her face in his big hands, the stroke of his thumbs along her cheeks infinitely gentle. "Take another chance on me, Mel."

"Oh, yes." He was worth every risk. "I meant what I said when I told you that I'd never get enough of you."

He chuckled, a devilish gleam entering his gaze as he tugged on the belt of her robe, unraveling the ties. "I'm holding you to that promise."

"Right here, right now?" she dared.

"Oh, yeah." Accepting her challenge, he pushed the heavy chenille off her shoulders and slid the thin straps of her gown down her arms, baring her to his hot gaze.

He palmed her full breasts, skimmed his fingers down to her belly. Having his hands on her again was pure heaven. Her hunger and need for him overwhelmed her, and she helped him to quickly undress, too, their urgency mounting with every scrap of clothing they removed.

They only made it as far as the couch, and he came down on top of her, naked and heavy, flesh to flesh, heartbeat to heartbeat. He branded her with his body, and possessed her in a single driving thrust that made them both shudder and gasp in pleasure. His arms went around her back, smoothed along her spine, wrapping her safe and secure in his strong embrace. She clung to the heat, the strength, the masculine scent that were uniquely his, and all hers.

He buried his face in her hair, his hold tightening as he let them both savor the thrill of their joining just a moment longer. "Damn, I missed you," he groaned.

She threaded her fingers through his silky hair, her heart content with the knowledge that she'd been on his mind, in his dreams, a part of his fantasies. "Did you *really* miss me?" she asked coyly.

"As much as it pains me to admit it, yeah, I did."

He lifted his head from her neck, which caused his lower body to arch into her, embedding him deeper. His eyes sparkled mischievously. "I need my secretary back."

Her jaw dropped open, and he chuckled, the deep, jovial tremors vibrating against her belly. "I missed *you*," he said before she could issue an indignant response. "But I most definitely need you back in the office. And I was thinking that I sure could use a partner every now and then on various cases."

"What's in it for me?" she asked impudently.

His hips moved and he slid into her, deep and slow, then out again. She moaned and wrapped her legs around the back of his thighs. "I give great bonuses."

She narrowed her gaze, remembering the last bonus he'd given her and how she'd felt about it. "I don't need money for something I *want* to do."

"Then I'm sure we can come up with a fair exchange. Your services for mine." He waggled his eyebrows rakishly and surged deep again. "What do you think?"

She'd never seen him so playful, so lighthearted, and she loved it. "I think you have yourself a deal." Before he could totally distract her with his lovemaking, there was one other issue they needed to resolve. "Cole...what about my father?"

He winced. "I don't think now's the time to bring

him into the conversation, do you? Unless you're looking to kill the mood."

She laughed lightly. "You're right, but talking to my father is something you're eventually going to have to deal with. He knows where I stand, but he deserves to know about us, and I think he ought to hear it from you."

"I know." He pressed his forehead to hers, their breaths mingling. "I have every intention of talking to him, but, right now, the only thing I want to think about is *you* and how great it feels to be back where I belong."

She sighed her agreement, and then all thought was lost as he kissed her long and slow and deep, shamelessly tempting and teasing her mind, her body, and senses...just as she'd seduced him from the very beginning.

_____Epilogue_____

"MELODIE, CAN I SEE YOU in my office, please?"

Cole made the request, disconnected the intercom and waited for his efficient secretary to enter. In less than a minute she arrived, gliding across the room confidently, the sexy skirt she wore giving him all kinds of wicked ideas. And, lucky for them, it was after six in the evening and Noah and Jo were gone for the day, leaving them completely and totally alone. Just as he'd planned.

The two of them had been dating exclusively for three months, and he couldn't imagine another woman in his life. Melodie was perfect for him, in every way. She matched him intellectually, stimulated him sexually and evoked a love so strong it threatened to consume him—in a good way. She never held back with him, not physically or emotionally, and it was her generous, selfless nature that allowed him to open up to her, too.

He'd never thought his life could feel so rich and rewarding, and he constantly marveled that this incredible woman was the reason. And, unbelievable as it was, she wanted him just the way he was.

She tipped her head as she neared, and he could tell by the diligent look in her eyes that she was expecting a business-related discussion. "What did you need?" she asked.

He grinned sinfully and crooked his finger at her. "I need *you*."

Her gaze softened with desire, and a sensual smile curved her lips. Rounding his desk, she slid onto his lap, entwined her arms around his neck, and brought his mouth down to hers for a hot, tongue-tangling kiss that stoked a fire deep in his belly. Knowing how easily one of these naughty office encounters could flare into a frenzy of passion, he reluctantly pulled his lips from hers before she ended up sprawled on his desk and his original intentions were forgotten.

She sighed dreamily, and her fingers played with the hair at the nape of his neck. "You know, the perks around here just keep getting better and better."

He chuckled. "I'm glad you think so. And speaking of perks, I've got a bonus for you, for a job well done lately."

She stiffened. "Cole—"

"Shh." Gently, he pressed his fingers over her damp lips, his eyes catching hers, silently asking her to trust him. "Don't refuse your bonus until you see what it is."

She sat quietly on his lap as he opened the side

drawer in his desk and withdrew the small, square, black velvet box he'd tucked there. She eyed the box warily and gasped when he opened the lid to reveal a glittering, one-carat diamond solitaire ring.

"Marry me, Melodie," he said, his tone gruff with emotion.

She pressed a hand to her breasts, her eyes shimmering with tears. "Marry you?" she croaked.

Panic surfaced, and Cole wondered if she'd grown content with their dating arrangement and didn't want the restrictions of marriage. "I never thought I could love a person the way I love you," he said, emphatically stating his case. "And I want everything that goes with it—commitment, marriage, living together under the same roof, waking up in each other's arms every morning."

"And what about having a family?" she asked, the question a cautious, tentative one.

He understood her reservations. He knew how much she cherished and valued family and wanted one of her own someday. While she might be willing to be his for the moment, he never doubted that someday the issue of children would be brought up between them. After thinking about the situation long and hard for the past couple of weeks, he was prepared to answer her question.

He drew a deep breath. "Yes, even a family. With *you*." He splayed his hand on her tummy, imagining her pregnant with their child, one created together, out of love. "Having a baby with you makes all the difference in the world.

He grinned. "I even went and asked your father for your hand in marriage. He gave me his blessing and said it was about time I made an honest woman out of you."

His fears with Richard had been unfounded. Cole had been nervous as hell when he'd approached the older man three months ago to tell him he was in love with Melodie, fearing disappointment, but Richard couldn't have been happier about the situation.

She laughed through watery, happy tears, her love for him shining through. "Oh, Cole," she breathed. "This is more than I'd ever hoped for."

"It's everything you deserve." Taking her left hand, he slipped the ring on her finger—a perfect fit, just as she was a perfect fit in his life. "Marry me, Melodie, and make an honest man out of me, too."

The ecstatic "yes" she whispered made his entire world complete.

* * * * *

Watch for Noah Sommers's story in

THE ULTIMATE SEDUCTION

Harlequin Blaze
November 2002

More fabulous reading from
the Queen of Sizzle!

LORI
FOSTER

with

Forever and Always

Back by popular demand are the scintillating stories of
Gabe and Jordan Buckhorn. They're gorgeous, sexy
and single...at least for now!

Available wherever books are sold—September 2002.

And look for Lori's **brand-new** single title,
CASEY in early 2003

Princes...Princesses...
London Castles...New York Mansions...
To live the life of a royal!

In 2002, Harlequin Books lets you escape to a world of royalty with these royally themed titles:

Temptation:
January 2002—*A Prince of a Guy* (#861)
February 2002—*A Noble Pursuit* (#865)

American Romance:
The Carradignes: American Royalty (Editorially linked series)
March 2002—*The Improperly Pregnant Princess* (#913)
April 2002—*The Unlawfully Wedded Princess* (#917)
May 2002—*The Simply Scandalous Princess* (#921)
November 2002—*The Inconveniently Engaged Prince* (#945)

Intrigue:
The Carradignes: A Royal Mystery (Editorially linked series)
June 2002—*The Duke's Covert Mission* (#666)

Chicago Confidential
September 2002—*Prince Under Cover* (#678)

The Crown Affair
October 2002—*Royal Target* (#682)
November 2002—*Royal Ransom* (#686)
December 2002—*Royal Pursuit* (#690)

Harlequin Romance:
June 2002—*His Majesty's Marriage* (#3703)
July 2002—*The Prince's Proposal* (#3709)

Harlequin Presents:
August 2002—*Society Weddings* (#2268)
September 2002—*The Prince's Pleasure* (#2274)

Duets:
September 2002—*Once Upon a Tiara/Henry Ever After* (#83)
October 2002—*Natalia's Story/Andrea's Story* (#85)

Celebrate a year of royalty with Harlequin Books!

Available at your favorite retail outlet.

HARLEQUIN®
Makes any time special®

Visit us at www.eHarlequin.com

HSROY02

If you enjoyed what you just read,
then we've got an offer you can't resist!

Take 2 bestselling love stories FREE!

Plus get a FREE surprise gift!

Clip this page and mail it to Harlequin Reader Service®

IN U.S.A.	IN CANADA
3010 Walden Ave.	P.O. Box 609
P.O. Box 1867	Fort Erie, Ontario
Buffalo, N.Y. 14240-1867	L2A 5X3

YES! Please send me 2 free Harlequin Temptation® novels and my free surprise gift. After receiving them, if I don't wish to receive anymore, I can return the shipping statement marked cancel. If I don't cancel, I will receive 4 brand-new novels each month, before they're available in stores. In the U.S.A., bill me at the bargain price of $3.57 plus 25¢ shipping and handling per book and applicable sales tax, if any*. In Canada, bill me at the bargain price of $4.24 plus 25¢ shipping and handling per book and applicable taxes**. That's the complete price and a savings of 10% off the cover prices—what a great deal! I understand that accepting the 2 free books and gift places me under no obligation ever to buy any books. I can always return a shipment and cancel at any time. Even if I never buy another book from Harlequin, the 2 free books and gift are mine to keep forever.

142 HDN DNT5
342 HDN DNT6

Name	(PLEASE PRINT)	
Address	Apt.#	
City	State/Prov.	Zip/Postal Code

* Terms and prices subject to change without notice. Sales tax applicable in N.Y.
** Canadian residents will be charged applicable provincial taxes and GST.
All orders subject to approval. Offer limited to one per household and not valid to current Harlequin Temptation® subscribers.
® are registered trademarks of Harlequin Enterprises Limited.

TEMP02   ©1998 Harlequin Enterprises Limited

eHARLEQUIN.com

community | membership

buy books | authors | online reads | magazine | learn to write

magazine

♥ ─────────────────────────────── **quizzes**

Is he the one? What kind of lover are you? Visit the **Quizzes** area to find out!

♥ ─────────────────────── **recipes for romance**

Get scrumptious meal ideas with our **Recipes for Romance.**

♥ ───────────────────────── **romantic movies**

Peek at the **Romantic Movies** area to find Top 10 Flicks about First Love, ten Supersexy Movies, and more.

♥ ─────────────────────────── **royal romance**

Get the latest scoop on your favorite royals in **Royal Romance.**

♥ ─────────────────────────────── **games**

Check out the **Games** pages to find a ton of interactive romantic fun!

♥ ───────────────────────── **romantic travel**

In need of a romantic rendezvous? Visit the **Romantic Travel** section for articles and guides.

♥ ─────────────────────────── **lovescopes**

Are you two compatible? Click your way to the **Lovescopes** area to find out now!

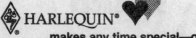

HARLEQUIN®

makes any time special—online...

Visit us online at
www.eHarlequin.com